CAPTURED BY THE FAE

Fate of the Fae

VERA RIVERS

Captured by the Fae:
Fate of the Fae - Book One

First printing, 2022

Publisher

Vera Rivers
vera@verariversauthor.com
VeraRiversAuthor.com

Cover art by: miblart

VERA RIVERS BOOKS

Receive a FREE romance ebook by visiting my website and signing up for my mailing list:

VeraRiversAuthor.com

By signing up for our mailing list, you'll receive a FREE ebook. The newsletter will also provide information on upcoming books and special offers.

"**G**et your hands off me!" I slapped a meaty hand off my ass, glaring at the offender.

He grinned yellow teeth at me. "What's holding up that beer, honey?"

"Touch me again, and you'll regret it."

"I don't think so. A sweet thing like you..." He continued touching me.

I'd had enough.

I moved fast. My elbow connected with his nose, and I felt a satisfying crunch. Blood poured from his nose and dripped onto his shirt while he howled.

"Let me get you that beer," I said through gritted teeth.

I would have asked him to leave, but it wasn't my call.

When I walked away, another male tried to grab me. I dodged the hand.

I wanted to spin around and punch him in the face, too. I hated it when drunk males slobbered all over me. I wasn't a piece of meat they could manhandle whenever they wanted just because I worked at the tavern.

I collected empty beer mugs and stayed clear of the really drunk guys.

"Do you want to tell me what the hell that was?" Craig demanded when I walked back to the bar to refill pint glasses with the bitter ale he sold on tap. His enormous, doughy belly strained against his stained shirt, in plain sight because of the two missing buttons, and his eyes were black, shifting in their little sockets.

He was in a mood today. I'd angered him since I'd come down from my room on top of the tavern at dawn this morning. I didn't know why.

He leaned on the bar, talking to some patrons while I ran around, running the show for nothing but the tips a few of them left, and a room with a daily meal I didn't have to pay for.

"He's groping me, Craig," I said and slammed the tray down so that the glass pints trembled. "He always gropes me, and you do nothing about it."

"No harm, no foul. He pays good money as a regular."

Yeah, I knew that. He was a regular *offender*.

"And if you're a sourpuss about it, you chase away my customers. One of these days, he's going to find somewhere else to spend his coin, and then? What happens if they all leave?"

"I'd be better off," I grumbled.

"What was that?"

"Nothing."

I'd been in a lot of fights, fending for myself when Craig refused to protect me. A tavern wasn't the type of place women worked when they wanted to be seen as respectable ladies.

Then again, Fae never saw human women as respectable. We were the slaves, the help, the bottom of the food chain.

Jasfin was Fae country. I'd heard that humans lived freely in the Uprain Mountains to the north, but it wasn't like I had the means to leave. On foot, it was more than a week's travel, and I couldn't afford it without my job here.

Even if I made it, what if I got there and they wouldn't have me?

I'd grown up being unwanted. My parents had gotten rid of me, my foster parents had used and abused me, and when I'd run away, this was the only place where I'd been able to take care of myself.

Besides, I'd lived my whole life—my *spectacular* twenty-one years—in Steepholde. It was a tiny town at the very south of the country bordered by a forest, with rolling fields and sunshine and the illusion of happiness. It was home. Whatever the hell that meant.

"If I catch you causing trouble with the patrons again, you're out," Craig threatened. "I mean it, Ellie. I can find someone to replace you tonight if I have to."

I stared at him, shocked. He'd taken away my meals, he'd forced me to work double shifts, he'd made me scrub the kitchen after hours. He'd never threatened my job. Craig didn't threaten.

When he said something, he meant it. That was why he was so terrifying.

"You can't do that to me!" If it was just a job, that would have been one thing, but it was my room, too. I wasn't going back onto the streets. I needed a roof over my head and food in my belly.

"It's my tavern. I can do whatever the hell I want. You humans think you can do whatever you want now that King Arnott is dead."

I bit back the snarky remark I wanted to throw at him. I clapped back often, but he was in a foul mood, and I couldn't risk my job. Not tonight. He was going to use the King's death on me for a while to come, still.

I'd read about the King's death, but the event didn't impact either one of us. A day of mourning had followed, where everyone was mandated to wear black and act like we were sad about a Fae no one knew personally.

The King was dead. Flyers of the murderer ruled every bulletin board, advertisement, and news bulletin. Blond hair, stern features, a face that looked like it was more comfortable with a snarl than a smile.

None of that affected us. It hadn't changed my life in the slightest.

Life was still tough all around. Rumors circulated that the new Fae King—Rainier, King Arnott's only son and next in line to rule—had plans to end slavery for the humans. The Fae complained about slavery being abolished, as if that would ever happen.

"You're treading on thin ice, Ellie," Craig warned.

I shook my head and filled the pints before carrying them back to the booths.

"Finally," Ham-Hands sneered and grabbed the pint from my tray before I handed it to him. He'd stopped the bleeding, but his teeth had blood on them when he grinned, and his eyes were filled with menace. He wanted to finish what he'd started now. It was a matter of pride.

He grabbed for me with his other hand, but I bounced back. I wanted to retaliate, put him in his place. I was small against his bulky size, but that meant speed would be on my side, and I was a decent fighter. Years of warding off assholes in the tavern did that.

But Craig was watching, and Ham-Hands was a regular customer. We couldn't risk those—or Craig's reputation—now, could we?

The last pint on my tray fell when I avoided his touch, and it shattered on the floor. Beer splashed everywhere.

"That's it," Craig said, standing.

I fell to my knees and started picking up the glass pieces, not caring that the glass cut my hands or that beer soaked my only pair of pants. I felt Craig's anger coming toward me as he stomped through the tall tables.

He grabbed me by the shoulder and yanked me back, planting me on my ass.

"You're not getting anything to eat tonight, you hear me? Do you have any idea what these cost me?"

Of course I knew. I was the one that always called in the orders.

"So, I have to feed everyone else, but I go to bed hungry?"

"You're not feeding them. *I* am. You're lucky you still have a place to sleep," Craig snarled and shoved me toward the kitchen behind the bar.

I shook my head and dumped the glass pieces into a bin on the way to the kitchen. When I was alone, I ran cold water over my hands, washing away the blood that seeped from the cuts created by the glass. I fought back my anger and blew the strands of auburn hair out of my face that had come loose from my ponytail. I tried not to think about the fact that I would not eat.

My stomach growled in protest.

I stayed in the kitchen, listening to the chatter and laughter die down as Craig greeted his patrons and closed up the front of the tavern. When he finally came into the kitchen, he ignored me. He opened the pantry and took out a loaf of bread, a chunk of cheese, and a bowl of salted butter. He added turkey to it from the fridge and locked it all up before he left so that I couldn't get anything for myself.

When he switched off the lights, I crept out of the kitchen in the dark and climbed the ladder to my room above the kitchen.

It wasn't much of a home, but it was better than sleeping on the street. I'd experienced a life of being homeless, and there was nothing I wouldn't do to avoid it. I slept on a pile of rags in the corner, on slivered wooden floors, but it was more comfortable than it looked. Aside from tonight's punishment, I usually went to bed with a full belly.

I twisted the ring that I always wore on my middle finger. It was the only thing I had from my mother—or at least that's what the woman who ran the orphanage told me. Maybe I twisted it hoping for some guidance, but really, I just twisted it out of habit. I took it off and placed it in my small box of personal possessions for safekeeping for the night.

I walked to the window and looked out.

Steepholde was a lot like the rest of Jasfin, from what I heard from travelers passing through the tavern. Everything was a combination of old buildings and traditions that stood the test of time and the latest technology. The digital lights, hologram advertisements, combined with the weathered bricks, slivered wood, and printed flyers was where the past and the future came together.

I sat down and put my arms up on the windowsill, looking out at the night. I tried to ignore how hungry I was. I tried to focus on the lights and the life teeming below—the push and pull between the Fae and humans living together. I wanted so much more. I'd always wanted more. I just didn't know what. I simply couldn't believe that this was it. This was what the rest of my life would be like. How was it possible that I, at twenty-one, had reached the pinnacle of my potential?

I didn't know how I would change my life, though—how I would get out of here. Being human in a world where we were *nothing* was a curse, and I had no way of changing my fate.

I wouldn't die of hunger tonight, but if I had to keep trudging through this mundane existence, I didn't know how I would keep on living. My soul yearned for more, yet it was never fed what it needed.

A sound from below snapped my attention back to the present. What was that? It had sounded like someone was in the kitchen, but...

I strained my ears for the sound again. This time, it was loud and clear. Someone *was* down there.

An icy finger trailed down my spine, and fear crept up from my core.

If someone broke in and stole something—anything—from Craig, I would get the blame—no matter what I did or said. I'd clapped back at him often enough. I'd put my foot down. I'd made life harder for him than I'd needed to because I hated being pushed into a corner. But he would take all this—pathetic as it was—away from me if something happened now.

I crept across my room, careful not to let the wooden floorboards creak, and climbed down the ladder. When I crept into the kitchen, the lights were off. I poked my head around the corner, tasting my heart in my throat.

Nothing.

I straightened and frowned. I could have sworn...

A scratching sound came from the storage room next to the kitchen. I spun around.

"Who's there?" I demanded.

Silence.

I took a step closer, and another. Again, the scratching sounded. I took a step into the storage room.

The whooshing sound of a large object swinging through the air came fast. An object hit my head. Hard. I swirled, but my vision was already blurry, and I barely made out a figure in the dark before everything went black.

　2　❦

I didn't kill the Fae King of Jasfin, but that was the first thing someone screamed at me the moment I woke up.

I opened my eyes, and nothing around me was familiar. I was lying on the ground, and the cold concrete seeped through my clothing and was frigid against my skin. My whole body involuntarily shivered. All four walls were metal bars, like a cage. Was I in a prison cell? Yes, I definitely was, and I had no idea why.

The same guard who had yelled at me from outside of the cell stormed in and forced me to my feet. My arms were chained, and the cold metal dug into my skin when the guard grabbed my wrist to force me forward.

"Move," he growled, and I obeyed.

The hallways and stairways he led me through were dark and cold, and the air was damp and smelled like mildew. A door opened, and there I was, in chains and standing in an arena of sorts. The stands rose like an amphitheater, and the crowds all around me were losing their minds with excitement. The electric atmosphere crackled on my skin.

Despite the sun beating down on the sand in the arena, a chill ran through me. The weight of the chains dragged me down. The magic of the spelled metal hummed against my skin. I would not work my way out of these chains. I had seen cuffs like this before—the magic was impossible to break unless whoever had cast it recalled it.

I tasted bile at the back of my throat. Blood rushed in my ears, and despite shivering with cold, sweat broke out on my skin, dampening my hair. I cleared my throat, and my voice was thick and...different. When I looked down at myself, I wasn't me. My body was enormous, muscular, the body of a man.

What in the seven realms of hell?

I wore a battle outfit, not my own clothes. But nothing here was my own—not even my body.

"Next!" a guard boomed.

Another guard pushed me forward, a spear at my back. The sand kicked up beneath my feet, and I tasted dust in my mouth.

Rainier, the Fae Prince, sat on the throne, his face stony, eyes filled with rage. I was just as confused as I was terrified. I was in the presence of the Fae Prince of Jasfin. He was a sight to behold, his pitch-black hair in stark contrast to his marble skin, and his eyes the color of ice. His gaze chilled me to the bone.

"Zander, I have charged you with the murder of the King."

Zander? I'd seen the flyers. I'd heard the name. But that wasn't me.

"I didn't do it," I said. My voice wasn't my own—it was deep and distinctly male. "You have the wrong person!" I fought against my restraints, but the spear dug into my back, and I stopped fighting. "I'm not—"

"I don't think so," Prince Rainier—or *King*, now that his father was dead—snapped. He would not let me finish. And why would he? I looked like this...like Zander.

His rage increased when he talked to me. His anger rushed toward me in hot and heavy pulses, laced with the sorrow of losing his father. It flowed through me like a cancerous ache, taking root. I *felt* the sadness buried at my core, threatening to drown me.

What the hell was going on? I'd felt nothing before but my own emotions. My own fear or rage. This was...wrong.

I glanced around, and no humans were in sight. I was in the middle of the Fae court.

me with red eyes and snapped its jaws. It was angry that I'd done damage.

This time, the creature seemed to calculate its next move. How smart was this thing? I was in trouble.

It backed away, tail flicking again. Those eyes locked on me and followed my every move. I waited. Storming the monster put me at a great disadvantage—I was only human. Or...whatever. In this body, I wasn't sure what I was. The monster was enormous, and I would let that count in my favor—or try to. Usually, I had speed on my side, but I was in a body I wasn't used to. I had to figure something out.

Dead was dead, no matter what body I was in.

When the beast charged again, I ran forward, too. I let out a vicious battle cry that sounded strange to my ears, coming from my mouth in such a deep bellow.

I saw the steps falter—the creature was unsure about my reaction. It expected me to curl away in fear.

Was I terrified? I was scared out of my mind, but backing down would only get me killed. I'd learned a long time ago the only way to win a fight was to give it my all.

When the monster hesitated, I took my chance. I leaped forward, spear pointed at the head. I tried to get it into the eye. The monster turned its head last minute, and the spear skipped off the scales and clattered to the ground on the other side of the large body.

I looked up, and the monster's lips turned upward, almost like a smirk. I held my breath, and terror froze me in place, but only for a second. I'd need to fight, or die a coward, and I wasn't one to give up so easily.

The beast crept closer. I was without a weapon and in trouble. I started backing away. This was exactly what I shouldn't do, but I had nothing to charge with now.

My back hit the wall, and I knew this was it. I was done. This monster was going to kill me, and I had no way to stop it. I glanced toward the hovel where we'd waited. It was too far for me to make a run for it. The guards poked their heads out, eagerly watching.

Everyone rooted for me to die.

Great.

The monster opened its jaws, let out a roar that made my bones rattle, and it snapped the giant mouth at my head. I ducked, and a deafening metal thud sounded. I blinked my eyes open and glanced up at the monster just above me.

It had gone for my head...and missed?

The crowd gasped. I looked at my hands and realized they were *my* hands. Whatever other body I'd been in was gone. I was myself again.

The only reason the monster had missed my head was that I was much shorter than the man I'd been a moment ago. I wore my own clothes again, so I could move more quickly in cotton pants and the loose-fitting tunic. The smell of the beer I'd kneeled in what felt like a lifetime ago rose to my nostrils.

I took the opportunity. I had to act fast. The monster didn't know what the hell was going on. Neither did I—no one did—but there wasn't time to ask questions. I was my usual size once more. Small and fast. I knew my body. I could trust it again.

I vaulted out from underneath the large belly of the beast. I rolled across the dust and found the spear gleaming in the sun. When I came up onto both feet, I crouched low, spear pointed at the beast.

It shook itself out and charged with an indignant roar—it was furious it was losing. And I was sick and tired of this. I just wanted to go home.

The thought was fleeting. I was stuck in a dream world, and I would wake up at any moment. If this monster killed me, I wasn't going to snap out of this nightmare, back home on the pile of rags where I slept. But still, I couldn't allow myself to give up to the beast.

Either way, this would be the end.

The monster lunged at me, and I dove forward into the same roll I'd used to get away from it. It put me between the creature's legs. Sharp claws scratched up the sand around me as it spun around, trying to reach me.

I yanked the spear up as hard as I could, slicing into the soft under-belly where there were no armored scales. Everything had a weakness. The leather skin tore open, and the monster screamed in agony as blood poured out. It splashed on my arms, hot on my skin.

I didn't have time to freak out. I tried to get another blow in, but the creature reared up on its hind legs and spun away from me, getting me out from underneath it. It knew I could do damage there.

It crouched low, and we were back to circling each other, stalking. The wound in its belly gaped and poured out blood, leaving a trail as the beast moved. I pushed my hair out of my face, long and red and in the way. The short men's cut I'd had a moment ago had been better for battle.

The creature was done with this back and forth, and so was I. I was getting tired. The strength I'd had in the male body was gone. I would lose if I didn't end this once and for all.

I didn't know what made me think I could do this, but I'd wounded the creature twice, and I still stood.

As if the monster was ready to finish this, too, it charged again. It limped slightly, trying to step around the pain in its belly. When the monster reached me, teeth bared, mouth open wide as if to swallow me whole, I used the spear as a vault. I ran forward and shoved it into the sand, jumping up. I thrust as hard as I could and ended up on the beast's elongated face. The teeth were below me.

The monster suddenly turned into a bucking bronco, trying to throw me off. I grabbed onto one of the spikes. It sliced my hand open, but I gritted my teeth through the pain and held on for dear life. If it threw me off, I would be dead.

The beast paused, only for a split second to orientate itself.

It was all I needed.

I grabbed the spear and shoved the tip into the monster's eye.

It let out a terrifying scream and reared up. I swung around, holding onto the spear. My body slammed against the monster's scales, and instead of shaking the spear out of the eye, the momentum and my weight shoved it in deeper.

The body went limp and sank to the ground, nearly crushing me. I had to roll out of the way.

When I came to a halt, a cloud of dust surrounded me, and I coughed. I pushed myself up and sank into a battle stance, in case the monster came again.

It was dead.

The lifeless body lay in a puddle of blood that oozed from the belly and eye and turned the sand into a thick, red soup.

When I looked up, the crowd was completely silent. They all stared at me in shock and awe. I gathered no one had killed a beast like this before.

A murmur broke loose as they muttered and mumbled to each other and to themselves. A few words traveled to me on the breeze.

She changed.

That was what they were staring at—not the beast, which I'd killed.

They stared at *me*. The man who'd turned into a woman.

I still wasn't sure how it had happened, or why. All I knew was that if it hadn't happened, or if it had happened a moment later, I would be dead now.

I ran my hand through my hair, the other hand feeling empty without the spear to protect myself.

The guards, who'd been staring at me from the hovel, suddenly snapped back to life and ran toward me.

I turned around, facing them, ready to fight whoever else was ready to take my life.

But the magic manacles snapped around my wrists before I could do anything. I looked at the guards, furious that they'd caught me yet again, but there wasn't anger or irritation or sheer disinterest in their eyes.

What I saw was fear. They were terrified of me.

I'd just killed their monster. They hadn't put the cuffs on me because they were worried I would escape. They'd chained me because they feared what else I would do.

4

A Fae male stepped into the arena, and he looked every inch a warrior. He was tall and thickset, with muscles for days. Cropped brown hair stressed his hard expression, and his green, merciless eyes tracked me when he walked to me.

"Come with me," he said.

I stared at him defiantly. I wouldn't do what he said. I didn't want to do what any of them said.

When I didn't move, he grabbed my arm in his giant hand and dragged me with him.

He was strong, but not only as a warrior. He had magic, too—more magic than any Fae I'd encountered in Steepholde. It flowed through me the moment he touched me. My muscles tensed, and I prepared to go another round. I had to get out of here, but his magic paralyzed me. I *wanted* to fight him. I couldn't do anything, though.

I *hated* magic.

He dragged me through the entrance he'd appeared from and up golden carpeted stairs. When we stepped under the roof, the cool breeze and shade brought relief after the scorching sun. I was filthy, sweaty, and covered in blood—the monster's and my own.

"Thank you, Dex," King Rainier said when the warrior—Dex—planted me, wobbly legged, in front of the King.

"Kneel," Dex ordered.

He didn't give me a chance to defy him again. He shoved me down, and my knees hit the ground.

"Your Highness," I said tightly.

"Look at me," King Rainier said.

I glanced up, and our gazes locked. Those icy eyes bore into the depths of my soul, and again, the world stopped. Everything faded away, and the two of us were removed to a different plane. His eyes swirled to become a brilliant azure and then a deep cerulean color.

"You're not Zander," he said, and his words sliced through the spell that seemed to hold us together. In an instant, his eyes changed back to the color of ice. His voice was deep, smooth like velvet, and a shiver ran down my spine. But his face was hard, contrasting with his warm voice.

I shook my head. "Obviously not."

"Execute her for treason," Lucia said. Her voice was sharp and unpleasant. "I don't know what her plan was. Maybe she tried to infiltrate and kill you, too, my love." She put her hand on his.

"Be quiet," King Rainier snapped.

He shook off her hand. He sat upright and tall, but he was stiff and unyielding.

The future Fae Queen looked shocked, but Lucia snapped her mouth shut. She leaned back in her high-backed chair rather than leaning toward the King as she had been. She folded her hands in her lap.

"What magic is this?" he asked me.

"I don't know. It's not mine."

"Then how did you shift back into your normal form?"

"Maybe *that* form isn't her normal form," Lucia interjected. "Maybe *that* creature is the trick."

I glared at her.

"Lucia," the King warned.

She pursed her lips.

"I don't know how it happened," I said.

"I want answers!" the King barked.

"Yeah? Get in line. You're not the one who had to fight for your life down there because someone mistook you for a murderer."

The King narrowed his eyes.

"Are you going to let her talk to you like that?" Lucia asked.

The King only glared at his betrothed to silence her this time before he turned his gaze back to me.

He was mistrusting. He didn't believe me. What was I supposed to do, *show* him I didn't have any magic? The fact that I couldn't show him any magic was exactly the point. I glanced at Lucia. She was unhappy he'd scolded her. But she was the submissive future queen, silent and ready to back her betrothed.

"My father is dead," King Rainier said with words filled with sorrow.

Once again, pain and sadness blossomed in my chest. I didn't know what to say. Everyone knew, but telling him that seemed harsh, even for me. His sadness stopped me.

"And you didn't kill him," King Rainier added. He curled his fingers around the armrest, his thumb drawing circles on the velvet padding. His left foot bounced lightly. His gaze was hard, but his eyes filled with uncertainty.

I shook my head. "I wouldn't know how."

The King raised his eyebrows. "I find that hard to believe. It looks like you're quite the fighter."

"When it's a matter of life and death, I'm going to fight. Was I supposed to sit back and let that thing eat me?"

Dex nodded next to me. I quirked a brow, surprised he agreed with me.

King Rainier regarded his warrior, his eyes thoughtful.

"Take her away," he finally said, waving his hand in the air.

Dex yanked me to my feet.

"What?" I cried out. "You're not letting me go?" Dex started dragging me away. "I didn't do anything! You can't do this to me!" I fought the hand that wrapped around my arm like a manacle.

"Wait," King Rainier said. Dex stopped dragging me away, and I turned to face the King. "Do you presume to tell me what I can and can't do?"

"You falsely accused me of being a murderer, refused to let me plead my case, and forced a punishment I didn't deserve upon me. I proved myself by killing that thing, and now you're just *discarding* me?"

Lucia gasped. "How dare you speak to your king like that! My love, I demand that you—"

King Rainier lifted his hand, silencing her. She bristled but snapped her mouth shut again.

"You're not the queen yet," he said in a cool voice. "I'll punish her as I see fit."

Lucia sawed her jaw open and shut, searching for words that didn't come. Her cheeks flushed scarlet, and her eyes filled with rage. King Rainier didn't seem too worried about her reaction. He turned his attention back to me.

"What is it you think I should do?" he asked.

"You're asking *me?*" I asked, surprised.

"You're the one pointing out how unfair I am."

Amusement filled his voice, although his eyes were still frozen. A new sensation filled me—an unexpected warmth coming from the King that had ordered me killed earlier.

"At the very least, you could apologize for being wrong about me," I said.

The King raised his eyebrows and looked at Dex, who shrugged his giant shoulder.

King Rainier laughed, and it was a beautiful sound—thick, velvety, smooth. It brushed against my skin, and I wanted to lean into it.

"I don't know who you think you are, but—"

"You didn't bother finding out, either," I interrupted.

The King's warm smile faded away, and those icy eyes pinned me.

"Do I have to remind you I'm the King?"

"The *Fae* king," I pointed out. "I don't serve you."

His jaw ticked. "No, but you serve the Fae, and they serve me. You're a prisoner. I could have your head for talking back to me at all."

I glared at him. It infuriated me that he'd treated me like this.

"You're supposed to be a just King. That's what they always said about you—the Fae who'd advocated for change since he was a young boy. Where is that king now?"

"Excuse me?"

"I know you challenged your father on everything." I balled my fists.

Dex gaped at me. Lucia looked torn between indignation and shock.

I continued. "The King that stands before me doesn't seem like someone who believes being fair is better than being feared. You just want to get rid of me—a pain, now that you didn't have your father's murderer, after all."

Everyone stared at me, stunned at my speech. I glared at the King, defiant, willing him to counter me.

"I will not apologize for this," King Rainier said tightly. "I don't know what magic is at play here, and until I do, you're to be regarded as a threat."

"So, what else is new?" He was getting over this—over *me*. And once the entire thing bored him, what would become of me?

King Rainier nodded to Dex.

"Take her away...to the High Priestess."

"Are you sure?" Dex asked.

"She'll be able to figure out what's going on here," the King said.

I opened my mouth to protest. Did I have no say in this? I'd been hexed, wrongfully accused, nearly killed, and they didn't want to hear my side of the story?

Before I could say anything more, Dex lifted his hand, and a spell danced from his fingers. It snapped my mouth shut as if he'd gagged me. I mumbled and fought the restraint, but magic was at work yet again.

Dex dragged me away. I glared back at the King before turning my face forward. Lucia, next to him, put her hand on his and said something in a low voice so that I couldn't hear.

I continued to fight the magical gag as Dex took me away from the arena with the crowds who had become restless after the action. They hadn't heard our conversation. We followed a path that led to the palace, and I noted where we were going so that I would find my way out when I broke free and ran. I would get my chance at some point. I *had* to.

All the while, I kept fighting the gag.

"If you fight it, it will just—"

The magic snapped, and I gasped.

"Are you still going to treat me like a prisoner, even when I did nothing?" I cried out.

Dex frowned. "How did you do that?"

"What?"

"The spell. How did you break it?"

I blinked at him. "Maybe I'm being a threat again," I sneered.

Dex pursed his lips together, his jaw clenched. Without him countering me, I had nothing more to say. We walked in silence. I was furious, but as my adrenaline faded, the anger gave way to uncertainty, and then to fear. My stomach turned, and my hands became sweaty.

"Where are you taking me?" I asked.

Dex marched me down a set of stairs and through an entrance that led into a large vestibule designed to hold many people.

"The High Priestess," he answered, telling me exactly what King Rainier had said. Clearly not the helpful type.

"And I don't suppose you could let me go," I tried. Dex only stared solemnly ahead. "Do you always do as you're told?"

He glanced at me, but he didn't say anything. He just kept walking, forcing me to follow.

The High Priestess. Maybe this female could give me some answers I needed. Like, how the hell I'd ended up here. And why I wasn't allowed to leave, even when I was innocent?

5

Dex led me down a long, narrow hallway with doors on all sides. He opened one door and gestured for me to step in. I hesitated.

"Is this where you keep her?" I asked, glancing into the bland little room.

Low ceilings made it feel cramped, and a cot stood in the corner. The windows didn't let in much light; they seemed shuttered.

"You'll wait here while I find her."

"No way," I said. "I'm not getting locked up *again*."

Dex clenched his jaw and grabbed me by the arm. I tried to fight him, but my strength was waning. My adrenaline had faded, and I was exhausted. He pushed me into the room—not without care—and pulled the door shut behind me.

"Let me out!" I shouted, grabbing for a doorknob, but nothing was on my side of the door.

"I'll be back for you," Dex said and walked away.

I listened to his footsteps fade. Then, I turned around, my throat swelling shut, and tears stung my eyes. It frustrated me. I would *not* cry. But hell, I was in a prison of sorts—yet again—and I was so tired of fighting.

I walked to the cot and sat down. It was narrow, and the springs creaked when I sat, but it was better than anything I'd slept on before. Exhaustion overcame me, and I couldn't think straight anymore.

Everything hurt. My muscles screamed at me, and I felt like I was one giant bruise.

What would happen to me? Was I to be a prisoner forever?

I lay back on the cot, my muscles protesting. As soon as my head hit the mattress, my eyes drooped shut.

The monster flashed before me, and my body jerked. I looked around, but I was safe. The monster was dead, its blood all over me to prove it.

I was still alive.

I didn't want to fall asleep. I had to stay on my guard, but sleep dragged me under, and I couldn't fight it. My body was giving in. Giving up. Eventually, so did I.

I didn't know how long I'd slept for. The sound of the door opening jerked me out of a deep slumber.

I sat up and rubbed my eyes.

"Come," Dex said. "She'll see you now."

"The High Priestess?"

He didn't answer.

When I stood, my body protested. My muscles were stiff and bruised. Moving was harder now that I'd cooled down and slept. I hobbled toward Dex, who turned and led me back down the hallway we'd come from. He took me to an unknown part of the palace.

I stared at everything around me in awe. I'd seen nothing like this —not even in some of the holo-ads I'd seen around town. I'd never read about anything like this in books.

The palace transcended earthly beauty. It was ethereal, and every- thing seemed to be kissed with gold. The marble floors had intricate flowers laid into them. I kneeled to study one of them. When I ran my fingers over it, it seemed like the flower was real, preserved against time by a sort of glue that gave it a shiny, magical appearance. The walls shimmered with a glittery substance that sparkled in the light that filtered through the windows. Depictions of battles adorned the high ceilings, with powerful warriors, beautiful damsels, and horses that bulged with power and pride.

"This place is incredible," I said, looking around me.

Dex only grunted something inaudible, that I assumed to be an agreement, and kept walking. Was he used to this kind of splendor? Did he recognize the incredible beauty for what it was, or was it run-of-the-mill to him?

After I'd grown up in squalor and filth and worked in bars where the males were dirtier than the floors they trod on, this place took my breath away. I was used to the color brown—everything in my life had been dirty. Nothing held pride in its very existence the way this place did.

The palace seemed to go on forever. We followed one long hallway after the next until we finally reached doors so tall, they nearly scraped the ceiling. The doors met in a sharp ogival arch at the center, and when Dex pushed them open, I realized they were stone. They scraped heavily along grooves in the ancient stone floor created by opening these doors again and again.

We left the beautiful fairy tale palace behind, stepping into a Gothic world of stone and candles. Light barely fought away the darkness. Whispers danced around us, and a strange fog curled in the corners.

Magic.

All of it was magic. We'd walked into some other realm.

At the end of the long hallway, we went into a large room. The windows were all designed with the same ogival arch. The ceilings were so high that I couldn't see them in the darkness, and a large fire roared in a fireplace at the far side of the room. Dark, neo-baroque couches huddled in a semi-circle, facing the fire.

"Dex," a soft voice sounded from one corner, and I noticed a large desk filled with scrolls and stacks of ancient parchments.

A female walked toward us, stepping into the light. She had the characteristic Fae features—pointed ears and shimmering skin. Her white flowing robes gave her the appearance of a goddess.

She glanced at me, and her gaze caressed me like a breeze. I fought the urge to back away. This Fae was powerful. I felt her magic dancing on my skin like a hot breath.

"I'm Nylah, the High Priestess of Jasfin," she said, introducing herself. She circled me, studying me, and it allowed me to study her, too.

She was beautiful. Ethereal. Chestnut hair hung below her waist. Her eyes were strangely golden and shimmering—like candlelight, but she wasn't reflecting the candles or the fire. The light in her eyes came from within. *Woah.*

"You can leave her with me," Nylah said when she'd circled around and stood in front of me again. "We'll find out what Ren needs to know."

Dex bowed again and turned.

"You're leaving me here?" I asked, and the panic was clear in my voice. I hadn't wanted to show fear, but her power made me nervous.

"Don't worry, child," she said softly, and her voice was soothing when she spoke. "I'm not here to harm you. My orders are from the King. If he sent you to me, you're quite safe."

I narrowed my eyes at her. "Who says he doesn't want to kill me?"

"If he did, you'd already be dead."

"He tried," I shrugged. "Too bad I wanted to live more than he wanted me dead."

Nylah shook her head and turned toward the couches that faced the crackling fire.

"Please, sit. Let's talk," she said.

Talk? This was far more civilized than the torture session I'd imagined. I followed her but stopped myself.

"I'm going to get blood all over your couches," I said. I wasn't bleeding anymore, but I was still filthy with blood and dirt, and the velvet couches looked like priceless antiques.

"Don't worry," she said. "Nothing a little cleaning spell won't fix. I want to talk."

Unsure, I sat down. I sank into the seats, and the weariness of fighting overwhelmed me. My body was heavy. I'd fought, but I'd changed shape, too. My nerve endings were raw, and I felt like a stranger in my own skin.

"Did Dex tell you what happened?" I blurted out. "Is that why I'm here? To be studied like some kind of freak?"

Nylah smiled at me, and her eyes were gentle. I wanted to trust her. It was a bad idea—I didn't trust anyone—but she exuded warmth and kindness, and I wanted to wrap it around me like a blanket.

"You're not a freak. You've been used. The King asked me to find out how and why. That's all we're going to do."

"How?" I asked. It didn't sound so bad.

"I'm the high priestess. I have access to powerful magic that others do not."

I nodded slowly. Nothing about her made me feel the urge to turn and run. I wouldn't have been able to, anyway. My body had given me all it could. I was done.

"Now, let's see what we can learn, so we can talk to the King, you and I." She held out her hand. "May I?"

I hesitated. I had a sudden urge to give her my hand, just as she'd asked. I wanted to please her, and I wasn't sure why. Her power resonated with something inside me I didn't understand, but I forced my body to remain still.

"What's your name?" she asked, dropping her hand, seemingly not offended that I didn't take it.

"Ellie," I said.

"Ellie," Nylah repeated, and she smiled. I liked the way she said my name with warmth in her voice. "How did you get here?"

"I don't know," I admitted.

"Okay. We're going to figure this out, but I need you to trust me. Can you do that?"

"After being thrown into an arena with a beast who wanted to kill me, being accused of the King's death, and being put in the body of someone else... Why not? What's the worst that could happen?"

Nylah chuckled. Her voice was like chimes on the wind when she did. "You have fire in you," she said. "Do you know who I am and what I can do?" she asked.

"You've already told me you're the high priestess, and I'm not quite sure what you can do. I know that you possess powerful magic, but that's about all." I knew it because there was no denying her power. I grew up and worked around Fae. I knew what magic felt like. I'd never felt power so strong before.

"That's right. You understand how the realms work?"

I nodded. I'd heard about it, but as a serving human, I knew very little about the heavenly realms. The Goddess Terra was the source of the Fae power and had breathed life into all beings. The high priestesses were in closer connection to her than the rest of the Fae, and closer than the mere mortals could ever be.

"The heavens have three realms," Nylah explained. "Our Goddess Terra resides in the Third Realm, which is all around us. She is all-encompassing and our source of power. High priestesses, like me, move in the Second Realm, closest to the Goddess, but once removed. I connect to her in some ways, finding answers that others may not, and hearing from her when there are questions that require answers she might see fit to give us."

I nodded. Judging by the power rolling off Nylah, it sounded right. I'd never heard it explained like this, but it worked for me.

"The First Realm is where the priestesses and the royal families live. They are above the Fae in power and status, closer to Terra, but not so close that they don't need me."

"And where do I come in?" I asked. "Somewhere under all of that, right? A bottom feeder."

Nylah's face changed from surprise to sympathy. "You're too hard on yourself. The humans live with a different belief system. It doesn't make you less important."

I didn't believe her. We lived in *their* world, so how didn't what the Fae believed apply? We were their slaves, or their workers. If nothing else, we shared the land.

"What we believe means nothing. It's all about you, the Fae, and what you need. That's what we're here for, right?"

She regarded me, and I couldn't read her expression. I was angry, frustrated, and scared.

"You've had a tough life," she finally said.

"Is there such a thing as a peaceful life for humans in Jasfin?"

"Not yet," Nylah said sadly, turning her face toward the fireplace.

Her sadness caught me off guard. "I know the humans don't have value to some Fae, but all life has value to me. That includes you."

"The King didn't think I had value," I spat. "He wanted me killed."

She nodded. "I know, but that was before he knew what you are, and who you're not. It's hard to see the world through fresh eyes when all you know is your pain, but it will bode you well to try."

I was angry. I wanted to get out of here. I wanted to go back to the world I understood. Nothing here made sense, and everything I tried to upset the High Priestess, to cause friction so I could fight my way out, failed. I was more comfortable with anger than with sorrow. I didn't want pity. I couldn't read her, and that was unsettling. I couldn't fight her, and that made me feel untethered.

"When I take your hand, I'm going to ask the Goddess Terra to show me what we're missing. If it's right, she'll share with us, and we can find out more."

"And if she doesn't think it's right?" As much as I respected the Fae deity, I wasn't sure what we were supposed to do if she was in a mood.

"She will reveal to us what we need to know when we need to know it."

It wasn't an answer. When someone didn't want me to know something, I would do what it took to figure it out myself.

I was out of my depth here. I was losing. Until I knew what the next step was, I had to be still and allow the High Priestess to figure out what had happened to me.

"May I?" Nylah asked again and held out her hand.

This time, I took it. I was still unsure, but I allowed it. I wanted to know as much as the King and Nylah did, and if she moved in the Second Realm and could ask the Goddess to show us what we wanted to know...what did I have to lose?

I put my bloody hand in hers. I was still filthy from the fight, and it looked so much worse against her pure cleanliness. But she didn't flinch or recoil when I touched her.

Nylah's skin was soft like the petals of a rose, and her power sighed along my arm, brushing against my skin and creating goosebumps on my shoulders.

She hummed a tune that sounded very much like an incantation or a chant.

"Goddess Terra, Divine Power, we call upon you this day to ask for a favor. We humbly approach you to ask what happened and how Ellie arrived to be among us. If you sent her here, show us how it came to be."

What if Terra *hadn't* sent me here?

I didn't have time to figure out the rest, to argue with what was happening, even if it was just in my mind. Suddenly, visions appeared before me, and it was like Nylah and I stood in the same room, watching the same reel. We still held hands, but the vision unfolded before us.

I watched myself as I worked in the pub back home, pouring pints of beer behind the old wooden bar, scratched over the years. Someone in a booth grabbed me. It was clear I didn't want it, but he continued harassing me.

I asked him to stop, as if words ever helped. When he didn't, I elbowed him in the face. Blood poured from his nose and blossomed on his shirt when he howled.

This happened all the time. Seeing my reaction objectively was impressive.

Nylah's tensed, and when I glanced at her, her mouth was open, the corners turned down. She was horrified.

We watched as Craig denied me my meal. I went to my room hungry and heard something downstairs. My heart beat in my throat when I watched myself going into the storage room. A shadowy figure knocked me out. Not with magic, but with a brick to the head.

I touched my head, feeling a bump. It had really happened. All this was true, although I didn't remember a thing.

The shadow started with an incantation that sounded similar to what Nylah had done, and before our eyes, my body shifted and changed until I'd taken the form of the man I'd seen reflected in the metal siding.

"A shape shifting spell," Nylah breathed. She'd seen this before.

The vision changed to where my male body lay on the floor in a cell. Guards came to take me away, and then I was in the arena, slaying the beast.

That was it. The vision disappeared as if someone had clicked off the projector.

"That's it?" I asked. "It didn't show how I got here."

"It didn't..." She looked deep in thought.

"Did the guards arrest me? Or did whoever that shadow was dump me here? Why can't we see?"

"It's all we get," Nylah said, letting go of my hand. She didn't wipe it on her white robes. Point for her—she was kind to me when she did not need to be.

"I don't get it," I said. "How does that help us? Does that mean Terra sent me here?"

"It means...we need to find out what's happening. But I firmly believe you're here for a reason, Ellie. The spell didn't hold up long enough to see you killed, and that's no coincidence."

"What does that mean?"

"Dex told me you broke the gagging spell."

I frowned. I didn't know what to say. My mind was foggy. I struggled to think straight. Maybe I was too tired. Or maybe the magic affected me like a drug.

"I'm glad the King sent you here."

I nodded slowly. "We'd learned very little. All I knew was that whatever Realm Nylah said she lived in...it had to be true."

"Why was I turned into a killer?" I asked.

"Zander," Nylah said.

"Yeah, the guy on all the flyers and in the news. He was a respected warrior in the King's court. I don't know what happened, or why he went rogue and killed the King."

Nylah nodded. So much still made little sense.

"Come, we must go to the King, now," Nylah said, standing.

I shook my head. "I'd rather not."

She smiled. "I won't let him hurt you. We must find out what happened. I will show the King what the Goddess showed us, and we'll take it from there. Come, child. You must trust that justice will be served. That counts for the innocent as much as it does for the guilty."

I swallowed. Nylah was easy to trust. Too easy. I didn't know why I put my faith in her when I knew nothing about her, but I liked her.

I followed her out of the large room, through the dark hallways, and back into the light, glittering palace. Despite the palace being lighter and brighter than the dark, Gothic cathedral, I'd been more at home back there than I was now.

Everything was so strange, and it kept getting stranger.

6

Nylah walked with me through the palace. Dex had marched me through the hallways like a prisoner, but with Nylah, I was a companion.

We strode through the palace, and again, I was in awe of how magnificent it all was. After my life in dark rooms filled with cinders and soot, this was a dream. A floral scent hung in the air, pleasing, intoxicating. We walked through a large gallery with oil paintings of the kings and queens past. My footsteps echoed around me in the wide space. I gaped at the paintings. They were to scale, every king and queen looking down at me as large as they'd been in real life, and although they were gone, I almost felt their looming presence.

"I like to visit them sometimes," Nylah said softly when she saw me looking. "They never really leave us."

"Really? That's...creepy."

She laughed. "Not like that. Their wisdom, their legacy, and what they meant to their kingdom stay behind, and that keeps their power alive.

"Is Lucia of royal blood?" I asked, thinking about the future Fae queen and how she'd sat next to King Rainier as if she was already on the throne.

"Noble, but not royal. She will marry into the First Realm when Ren takes her as his wife, and then she will inherit the power that comes with it."

"I thought only royals could marry other royals," I said.

"If there are others who are eligible. Otherwise, one of noble blood may be chosen. Lucia's mother is a priestess, and she also moves in the First Realm, which makes Lucia a perfect match for the King."

We reached a large, ornately carved door with a floral design chiseled into the ancient wood. She lifted her hand, but before she knocked, a voice called from the other side.

"Enter."

Nylah opened the door, and we stepped into the room.

Like all the other rooms in the palace, this one was large, with high ceilings. A French window stretched from floor to ceiling on the one side of the room, and full-length bookcases covered the opposite wall. A large desk was front and center in the room, not unlike the desk Nylah had been sitting behind.

King Rainier stood in front of the tall windows, looking out, his hands clasped at his back.

"Nylah," he said when he turned, and there was an easygoing kindness in his voice. When his blue eyes fell on me, the kindness disappeared. "What news?"

"I found little, but what I found might help you decide what to do with our guest."

Nylah didn't refer to me as a prisoner. That was nice of her.

"Okay," the King said. "Show me."

Nylah walked to him and kneeled before him, showing respect before she stood and took his hand, her right to his, so that it looked like they were shaking on something. She closed her eyes, and the power she possessed filled the room. It spilled into the corner of the office. A moment later, the King's power joined hers. It was so strong, the room threatened to burst open at the seams. I struggled to breathe.

They said King Rainier was one of the most powerful Fae to ever exist. I'd always thought the people who said it had some kind of power envy or were starstruck. But now that I felt what he could do, I was convinced they were right.

Nylah and the King stood locked together for some time. I watched them, but I was uncomfortable, like I was witnessing a private moment. I walked to the tall windows, careful not to make a sound.

The view was beautiful. The windows overlooked a valley with trees and a river lazily winding along the path the foot of the mountain provided. Everything was lush and alive. Along the river, I noticed beautiful houses dotted between the trees. They belonged to Fae, with humans for servants who had it hard even when they lived between lush trees.

"All right," the King finally said, and the power subsided. When I turned to look at them again, they'd let go of each other's hands. "And you think she'll be an asset?"

He asked Nylah the question as if in response to something she'd already said, although neither of them had spoken a word since they'd taken hands.

"I do. Her warrior-like abilities will come in handy," Nylah said.

Of course, she'd had that vision. I'd seen it, too. She'd seen me slay the beast.

King Rainier nodded and turned to me.

"You have a choice, Eleanor," he said.

"Ellie, please." Being called Eleanor made me feel small—it was the name my parents had chosen for me, or at least that was what I'd been told. Those parents had abandoned me, so I didn't like using my formal name.

"Ellie..." He walked toward me, and when he came closer, I *felt* him. Up close, without the hostility of thinking I was a killer and sentencing me to death, I was even more aware of how incredibly handsome he was. His features were celestial. It was the only way to describe it. He was like a god, and I suddenly wondered what his skin would feel like beneath my fingertips.

"What?" I asked, clearing my throat, willing him to say something —*anything*—so that I could stop thinking things I had no business thinking about a Fae King.

"If you wish, I will allow you to go back to the life you lived before.

You will leave here a pardoned woman, with no mark to your name. I'll forget this nasty business, and you will be free."

"What's the other option?" I asked carefully.

"You can stay here at the palace—I will give you quarters of your own—and you will train to become a warrior in my elite guard."

"You want me to fight for you?" I asked, surprised. "I'm just a human."

It was well known that the few humans who had the chance to work for the royal family did nothing that mattered. Important jobs were reserved for the Fae, and that included the warriors. How could powerless humans fight against the Fae when it came to war?

"You're right," King Rainier said. "But your skills are impressive. No one has killed the Farynx the way you did—not even the Fae."

I assumed the Farynx was the creature I'd killed.

"I believe you'll be an asset to my team, but I won't force you to stay against your will."

He would let me go if that was what I wanted. I blinked at the King, trying to bring the hostile male from earlier together with this reasonable monarch. Maybe Nylah's vision had done more than show him the truth. It had softened him, too.

The High Priestess seemed to have that effect on those around her.

But what he offered was an easy decision. My life in Steepholde had been awful. I'd been worthless my whole life—abused, harassed, and my job at the pub barely paid enough to stay alive. Males groped me, females despised me, and I'd had to fight for survival every day for as long as I could remember. Here, I would have quarters of my own. Training could amount to a better life, a future.

"What makes you think I want to stay somewhere I was accused of murder?" I asked.

Was I being ungrateful? Yes, yes, I was. But I didn't want to defer to the King, even if his position commanded it. He hadn't even cared about my side of the story.

"You've been pardoned," he snapped.

"Gee, thanks."

"I'm offering you a very comfortable life, Ellie," the King said, with narrowed eyes. His frustration washed over me. Whenever I was around him, I felt his emotions. It was unnerving, and I forced myself to think straight, to keep challenging him. Anger and fighting grounded me. Sad, but true.

"What you're offering is a half-hearted attempt to make up for nearly killing me when I'm innocent."

King Rainier looked at Nylah, exasperated. A non-verbal conversation passed between them.

"If you want to leave, I'll let you go," he finally said. "It's nothing to me, either way."

I narrowed my eyes. I didn't believe it. I didn't *feel* it from him. It didn't matter what he thought, though. What mattered was where I would end up. I was the only person I had to look out for, and I would do what it took to survive.

I wasn't going back to the tavern, that was for sure. Here, I *would* have a better life. It couldn't be worse than living and working at the tavern. But here, I might find answers, too.

"I'll stay," I said.

The King smirked. "Wise choice. Your training starts tomorrow."

"Come, Ellie," Nylah said. "You will need to get settled. I think you'll be very happy here."

She turned, and I followed her to the door. Just before we left, I looked over my shoulder at the King, but he'd turned his face to the windows again. I couldn't tell what he was thinking.

7

Dex was sullen and serious as he led me to the warrior quarters on the far side of the palace.

We walked in awkward silence. I was going to join Dex's ranks eventually. How did he feel about the fact that I was human, joining the King's elite guard? I couldn't gauge his reaction when Nylah had summoned him to lead me to my new room.

I got the feeling talking wasn't one of Dex's strengths.

"What is the training schedule like?" I asked, trying to make conversation.

"Rigorous."

"Right, right. I mean, because we'll have to be in peak condition."

Dex only nodded.

"Do you think I'll fit in with the others?" I asked.

He glanced sidelong at me. "Don't know."

"You don't talk much," I said.

"Not much to be said," he answered, and I stopped trying to initiate any conversation.

We turned down a long hallway—it seemed to be mostly what the palace comprised—and Dex led me to a door almost at the end.

"This is you," he said and pushed the door open. "Training starts at the crack of dawn. Be ready. Meals are served in the mess hall. You're not to leave the grounds unless the King orders it so. If you do, we'll consider it your resignation from the position."

"That's...harsh. What about leave to see family?"

"Do you have family?" Dex asked.

His words sliced through me. I didn't have anyone at all. I'd been orphaned as a baby, lived in an orphanage, and then I was adopted into a family that abused me.

I ignored the question and walked into the room, and Dex shut the door behind me.

They were right to call it *quarters*. It was nothing like what I'd had before.

My quarters consisted of a bedroom, with a double bed and an armchair that faced the window. A large wardrobe held various items of clothing. I wasn't sure if any of them would fit me.

A small reading corner sat adjacent to the bedroom with a chaise and two tall bookcases filled with books of all kinds.

The bathroom was big enough for a full bath, a shower with waterfall spray, and counters that housed the basin and stretched along the one side of it with mirrors above it.

I glimpsed myself in the mirror and winced. I looked terrible, with blood caked on my body and ripped and stained clothes. My blue eyes were dull and lifeless. I definitely needed sleep. Bruises mottled my arms and neck where the monster must have done a number on me, and cuts riddled my hands. During the fight, adrenaline had been pumping far too hard for me to feel any of this.

Nylah had met me like this. And so had the King in his office.

I squeezed my eyes shut. Awful.

"My lady," someone said from the door.

I turned.

A servant stood in the doorway. She donned a simple gray frock, and she wore her mousy hair in a low bun. But her face was open, and her eyes bright. She was human, like me, with a round face, unlike the Fae's sharp features.

"I'm Bessie," she said. "I'm here to see you're taken care of."

"Oh. I'm Ellie."

Bessie nodded. "We know who you are."

"You do?"

"Word travels fast. You're the male who changed into a woman and slayed the King's Farynx."

I swallowed. "Hell of a first impression, huh?"

A smile played around her mouth. "One of the most memorable first impressions, my lady."

"Please, call me Ellie." Being addressed as if I had rank made me uncomfortable.

"I don't think so," Bessie said. "Shall I lay something out for you to wear?"

I hesitated. "Do all warriors have servants assigned to them?"

"Yes. But I volunteered to take care of you, my lady."

"Really? Why?"

Bessie nodded. "The others were afraid."

"Oh." My stomach dropped.

"I'll lay out your clothes."

I nodded, and she left the bathroom. I wasn't sure if I should be offended.

I turned on the shower. The water was hot instantly, warmed by magic. I stripped off my clothes and stepped under the spray. The water turned red with the blood running down the drain, and my cuts stung when I applied soap, but I scrubbed myself until I was clean. I washed my long red hair until the water ran clear—the blood was less visible on my locks—and finally, I wrapped myself in the softest towels.

I'd always had to make do with a bucket of cold water, and soap had been a luxury I'd rarely had.

This was divine.

Bessie stood in the corner like an ornament when I walked to the wardrobe with a towel wrapped around my body. I glanced out of the large windows. The warriors' quarters formed a half-circle, all of them looking out over training grounds. Various arenas lined up next to each other with different equipment and dummies and running track and targets.

None of the arenas were where I'd fought the monster. I was glad. I didn't want to set foot in that place again.

"What are the warriors like?" I asked.

"Unrefined, my lady. Rough. But dedicated. They're a tight-knit group, a family."

At the word 'family,' my stomach twisted.

"The elite guard is a special group of Fae. You should be honored to be joining such ranks," Bessie added.

"Elite guard?" I'd heard about this unit of the King's military—the best of the best. "I thought I was just training to be a warrior."

"Oh no, my lady. You've been assigned to the elite guard."

My stomach tightened in a knot of nerves just thinking about it. I'd always fought my way out of trouble; I could take care of myself just fine. But being part of an elite group of fighters, and being formally trained, was different.

"I don't have magic," I said.

"I wouldn't worry about it, my lady. You're here by order of the King. The warriors on the elite guard won't counter his decision."

"I'm human."

"A human who slayed the Farynx."

I glanced at her. My reputation preceded me. Was it a good thing?

I turned away from the window. Tomorrow, I would get a taste of what it was all about.

Bessie had laid out a cream dress, simple and elegant, with long sleeves and material that was lighter than air when I pulled it on.

"This dress is my size."

She nodded. "The King arranged a wardrobe for you."

I opened the closet and studied its contents—outfits for training, casual wear, and long robes.

"If you'll take a seat, my lady." Bessie gestured to a dressing table opposite my bed. "I'll help with your hair."

"I can do it myself." I'd been akin to a servant my whole life. Being served by a human when I was one of them was unsettling.

"The King commanded me to take care of you."

She offered me a determined look. I hesitated before I sat down. Bessie picked up a brush and combed my wet hair out before drying it with a dryer. She braided it down my back while I watched her in the mirror. Her fingers were skilled, her lips pinched together in concentration.

When she finished, I turned my face this way and that.

"That's really pretty," I said.

Bessie smiled. "I'm exceptionally skilled with hair."

A knock sounded on my door. When I opened it, another servant stood before me, dressed the same as Bessie, her hair styled in the same low bun. She bowed her head.

"The King requests an audience," she said.

"Oh, right now?"

She nodded. "I'll show you the way."

I glanced at Bessie, who nodded encouragement.

I followed the servant through the maze of hallways. It was going to take a while before I knew my way around here. This place was a labyrinth.

Finally, she led me into a dining room. Empty plates stood on the table, but only the King was present. He sat at the head of the table. When we walked in, he looked up.

Was I supposed to bow? I wasn't sure, so I tried to curtsy, which probably looked like an inelegant squat.

The King smirked, and the servant snorted, but she quickly tried to cover it with a cough.

"Ellie," he said. His voice was cold. "Come in. Are you hungry?"

I started shaking my head, but my stomach rumbled, contradicting me.

"Bring her food," he said to the servant, who hurried away. "You missed supper in the mess hall, I imagine. You'll eat here. Dex informed you about tomorrow?"

"To be in the arena at dawn," I said, nodding.

"Good. Breakfast is before that. Eat well. You'll need your strength."

I was used to an early start, but eating before dawn was going to be a challenge. I nodded. I would do what I needed to stay here.

King Rainier stood, and I watched him as he paced the room. His stature was upright, his manner proud. He walked like a male who knew how to handle himself. I didn't doubt that he could. I doubted he was the type of warrior to lose in a fight.

"You won't fight with the others for a while. We'll need to get you up to speed."

"I can handle myself," I said.

"Yes, apparently, you can."

Heat rushed to my cheeks. "What I mean is, I don't need to be singled out. I can get up to speed."

"You're not Fae, Ellie," King Rainier said.

I groaned inwardly. I was aware of my limitations.

"I know, but I can make up for my lack of magic with my fighting skills."

"Your style is rough, unrefined. You need a lot of work, but you'll get there."

I bristled at his hard remarks.

"I'll prove myself worthy," I said with a clenched jaw.

King Rainier turned to me, and his expression softened. His eyes became drowning deep, the color of the ocean rather than the cold ice in his gaze, and my heart skipped a beat. I forced myself to look unhindered, but his effect on me was jarring.

Damn it, he was the King, he was taken, and he'd tried to have me killed. If there ever was a red flag situation, this was it.

Keep it together.

"I'm sure you will," he said.

His eyes were warm, but behind them, sorrow lurked like a beast that waited to devour him.

For just a moment, I saw the male behind the mask. He was a king and powerful Fae, but he was also a being with feelings. And he was hurting. As if my thoughts had opened a floodgate between us, I tasted his sorrow on my tongue. It tasted like the first spring rain, and it was so intense, it made me sad, too.

The door to the dining room opened, and Lucia stepped in. Her long blonde hair had been pinned up in intricate curls, and it glittered with gems and jewels. She wore a tight dress that revealed her narrow waist with a neckline so low, it left very little to the imagination. Her skin shimmered when she moved, and she reminded me of a goddess.

I watched King Rainier close off and *felt* a door slamming shut when she walked in.

"I thought you were meeting me on the terrace," Lucia said in a bright voice.

"I had business to take care of."

Lucia looked at me down her nose like I was a bug that needed to be squashed, and she pursed her lips together.

"Well, don't take too long," she said, looking at the King again, and she smiled coyly. She fluttered her eyelashes at him, leaned in, and kissed him.

I cringed and turned away. I couldn't stand the sight of her with him. I couldn't put my finger on what bothered me. I didn't like Lucia. Beautiful on the outside, but grotesque on the inside.

When she left the dining room, King Rainier sighed.

"Do you have questions?" he asked.

I wanted to know what he saw in her and if he was happy about the match. He seemed so sad. How could he be happy with someone they'd forced him to marry?

But then, he'd recently lost his father. His pain was going to last for a while, still.

I shook my head.

"Good," King Rainier said. "If you do, plenty of Fae are around who will be happy to help you."

The door opened yet again, and the servant girl returned. She had a bowl of soup on a tray and a plate of freshly baked bread with butter that melted from the heat.

My stomach rumbled again.

"I'll leave you to it," King Rainier said. "Enjoy your meal."

He left the dining room, and the servant girl followed. He left me alone in this grand room, with the chandelier over the dining room table, the glittering walls, and the large French windows that showed only darkness outside now.

I sat on one chair, picked up a slice of bread, and bit into it.

I groaned with delight and scarfed down the rest of the food.

❧ 8 ☙

Incessant beeping ripped me out of a deep sleep. It took me a moment of panic to realize the beeping came from a holographic clock displayed on my nightstand.

I sat up and rubbed my eyes. It was still dark outside.

The door opened, and Bessie walked in.

"Good morning, my lady," she said with a smile. "I trust you slept well."

"I could have done with an hour or two more," I grumbled.

She didn't answer. She walked to my closet and chose an outfit for me to wear.

"You must hurry. They will serve breakfast in half an hour. If you miss it, you won't eat until lunch." She peeled back my bedding when I didn't get up. "Come," she urged.

I got up and stretched. My body ached after the fight yesterday.

I changed into the clothes Bessie had laid out—black leather pants and a matching top with no sleeves. Silver thread embellished the chest and the hem of my pants. Despite the material, the outfit was comfortable, and when I tested my movement, I found it was unrestricted.

Bessie urged me to sit down at the dressing table, and she braided my hair again, tying it back so it would stay out of the way when I trained.

"You must hurry to the mess hall," she said when she was done. "Quickly, my lady."

I hurried to the mess hall. When I approached, the low hum of conversation filled the hallway, but it stopped abruptly when I stepped through the double doors. Everyone turned to look at me.

I swallowed hard.

"A tray, my lady," a servant said next to me, and I jumped slightly before taking it. She showed me where to go, and I walked to the human who was serving breakfast from a series of metal dishes.

"Anything you'd like, my lady," he said.

I chose honeyed oats and a piece of fruit. Eating in the morning was a foreign concept.

I turned and surveyed the room. The heavy wooden tables were all filled with warriors who ate. They'd continued talking after I'd walked in, but I was painfully aware of them watching me.

A warrior sitting alone at a table waved at me and beckoned for me to join her. I walked to her and sat down.

"Farynx Slayer," she said.

"Ellie."

She grinned. "Zita." Her blonde hair was cropped short, with a longer fringe swooped to the side. She was tall and powerful and exuded confidence. Her sharp features, shimmering skin, and pointed ears screamed Fae. "You're a legend around here, killing that thing. The King loves that Farynx. You killed his favorite pet."

"He shouldn't have put me up against it if he loved it so much," I countered.

Zita laughed. "Feisty, aren't you? Relax, I'm kidding."

Tension left my body, and I took a bite of the oats in my bowl. I groaned and dug in.

"It's not *that* good," Zita said, watching me devour my breakfast.

"You don't know," I said with a full mouth.

She laughed and shook her head, finishing her own oats.

"Word of advice," she said. "You're a warrior. You're not like the rest of us, but if you don't act the part, they'll treat you like an outsider. You're one of us, so *be* one of us."

She stood, and I watched her walk away with sure steps.

I glanced around. The others were still watching me from the corner of their eyes.

I straightened a little and finished my breakfast, too.

"YOU'RE ON TIME," NYLAH SAID, STEPPING OUT OF A SIDE DOOR that led directly from the palace.

I stood in the arena, ready to get to work. The sun was a red orb on the horizon, bleeding color into the night-stricken world, and Nylah looked as fierce as any other warrior I'd seen in the mess hall this morning.

I nodded. "I don't want to mess this up."

She smiled and walked to me. She'd pulled her long chestnut hair into a tight braid so that her golden eyes looked like the midday sun. Instead of her long, flowing robes, she wore leather clothes, similar to mine. Hers were white, rather than black, and embroidered with silver thread.

"How did you sleep?" Nylah asked.

"Oh..." I wasn't used to being asked how I was doing. "I slept well."

Actually, I'd slept like a baby. The bed was softer than anything I'd ever slept on, and the silence in the warrior quarters had been divine.

"That's good. You'll need your strength for our training sessions and the battles you'll eventually fight in. I suspect you're tired, but time will fix that."

I liked Nylah. Despite her terrifying power, she was warm and welcoming. I was a human, but she treated me like I was Fae.

Around here, they all did.

"Let's get started," she said. "You're at a bit of a disadvantage, since you don't have magic of your own, but that doesn't mean you won't be able to protect yourself." She thrust her hands at me, and a wave of magic hit me, making me stumble.

"Did you feel it coming?" she asked.

I shook my head.

"I'm going to do it again. I want you to focus on what you *feel*—not what you see me doing. Not anything other than what's going on around you."

She did it again. This time, before the power hit me, I felt it coming. It was like a blast of heat that tried to engulf me. I tried to side-step it, but it followed me and hit me anyway.

"You can never outrun magic, Ellie," Nylah said. "It will catch up with you—every time. Come." She walked to me and took my hands. "I want you to close your eyes and turn your focus inward until you find your center." I closed my eyes and did as she asked, but the concept was strange. My center? Was it my heart? Or my stomach? How was I supposed to know what that meant?

"Stop thinking so hard," she instructed. "It's going to trip you up. Thinking is what gets us all killed."

I gasped.

"A painful truth, I know, but let me take you there. Stop thinking...and just feel."

I tried to do what she said, and I sensed Nylah. I felt her presence, as if she wasn't in front of me, not physically. She pulled me down, as if she turned my consciousness inward.

"Now," she said. "Stay there."

I kept my eyes closed. She let go of my hands, and it took all of my focus to stay where she'd taken me. When another wave of magic came, I not only felt it much better than before, but it bounced off me, or flitted around me. It did nothing to me.

"Oh, wow," I breathed.

Nylah chuckled. "It's going to take time and practice to get there without thinking at all, and to stay there while your eyes are open and you're actively fighting. I want you to practice it. Meditation in your room when you have quiet time will help. We're going to work on it when we train, too. You want to look after yourself, and that's the only way a human can do it."

I hadn't known humans had an ability to face the Fae. I'd always thought we were the lowest on the food chain, and that was the end.

Nylah and I worked for the next hour, focusing on getting to that point where I could counter basic magic when it came at me. By the time the hour was up, my head ached, and I was mentally drained.

Dex appeared and watched us work for a moment before Nylah nodded, acknowledging him. He stepped forward.

"Dex will train you for a while," she said. "You did well. I'll see you a bit later."

I nodded, nervousness settling in my gut. I was getting comfortable with Nylah, but Dex was large and strong, and he wielded magic along with it. He was extremely powerful, which is why I assumed he was the general of King Rainier's military.

I'd faced males his size before, though. I'd faced them and won. I knew what I could do.

I squared my shoulders and glared up at him. I would not let him get me down. He had magic, but that wasn't new to me, either.

Nothing was, and yet everything was as well.

He stood in front of me and started running me through drills. If I thought I was tired after my training with Nylah, Dex wore out my body until my legs trembled, and I worried that if I took one more step, I wouldn't be able to stand.

"You're weak," he said when I sat in the sand in the middle of the training arena, drinking water like my life depended on it.

"Thanks for the compliment," I gasped through gulps.

"You're going to need a lot of work before you're ready."

I poured water over my face and hair, trying to cool down. The sun had become hot, and the leather clothing I wore did *not* help matters in the heat.

"That's what I'm here for, right? From prisoner to warrior. Suddenly, I'm trusted to sleep under the same roof as the King."

"You've done nothing wrong."

"That's stopped none of the kings before," I pointed out.

The Fae kings had never been known for their mercy. They could lead a country to thrive, but cross a king, and you died. End of story.

Dex clenched his jaw. "King Rainier won't follow in the footsteps of his father."

I studied him. He was a male of few words, solemn and quiet, but he looked like he cared about King Rainier.

"Are you friends?" I asked.

Dex blinked at me. "We've been close for years."

How was someone close to a male who barely talked? Maybe Dex was different around the King.

"The death of his father must be hard on him," I said softly.

Memories from the previous night came back to me. The sorrow in the King's eyes had laid in wait for him to drop his guard, so it could overpower him. The way he'd crumbled beneath the surface, a sensation I'd felt rather than seen, had stayed with me. I'd felt his pain more than once, now, even when he patched himself up and put on a face for Lucia.

"The King has to deal with a lot," Dex admitted. "There is a lot of pressure on him, not only because he mourns, but pressure to be different, and to do the right thing."

I nodded slowly. My heart went out to the King. I couldn't imagine what it had to be like to lose a father. I'd grown up without family and yearned for a life with someone warm to care for me. To have that, only to have it ripped away...

Dex cleared his throat. "You should change and eat lunch. The High Priestess will meet with you in the cathedral after you eat."

He'd closed up on me again. But he'd talked to me. The ever-solemn Dex had a soft side to him, too.

I grinned at him. "That was quite a speech. Warming up to me, huh?"

He rolled his eyes before his solemn mask fell back into place.

9

When I jerked up in bed the next morning, the holographic clock on my nightstand told me it was almost an hour after I should have been up.

"Oh, Goddess, no, no," I muttered as I yanked fresh training clothes onto my body and ran to the arena. I had no time to eat or shower. I would do that later.

When I skidded into the arena, Dex had a scowl on his face, and Nylah stood next to him, arms folded and lips pursed.

"Do you think a war will wait for you to sleep in?" Dex snapped when I arrived. "Do you think your fellow warriors will pick up your slack and die for you? When you demand this kind of luxury, someone else has to pay for it."

With eyes wide, I shook my head. "I'm sorry. I overslept. I'm not used to—"

"This isn't a game, Ellie!" Dex shouted. "Either you want to be here, or you don't. This isn't a hotel where you come and go as you please. When I say you're in the arena at the crack of dawn, that's what you do."

He turned on his heel and marched away. My stomach dropped,

and my throat tightened. Did no one around here make mistakes? I couldn't fail. Not now that my life had finally turned around. If they sent me back...

Nylah stepped forward. Her face softened when she looked into my eyes.

"You should see it as a compliment," she said.

"How? This is my second day! I'm still getting used to all of this. It's not like I'm trying to be difficult."

Nylah nodded. "I know, but the standard here is very high. You're training to be a part of the King's elite guard. It's not a title that you should take lightly, and Dex wants you to be at the top of your game. He thinks you can do it, or else he wouldn't have gotten mad. Focus on that."

I nodded. I would try to see it that way, but it was hard not to feel lower than low after how I'd let myself down.

"Come, let's focus," Nylah said.

We tried to work on the same meditation and focus as the previous day, but I was upset, and it was hard to sink into my center. When Nylah threw her magic at me, I didn't only stagger or stumble. The magic rolled me, threw me against a wall, tossed me across the arena, or slammed me into the ground.

"Focus, Ellie!" Nylah encouraged.

"I'm trying!" I shouted. "You're using too much!"

"It's the same as yesterday. You just need to focus."

I tried, but the magic beat me every time—physically and mentally. The more the magic whipped me around, beating me up, the more upset I became, and it was like a vicious cycle.

"This won't work," Nylah said, and all the power sucked out of the arena as if it had never been. "You're too upset."

"I wonder whose fault that is," I snapped.

She raised her eyebrows.

"I'm sorry," I muttered.

This was my fault. I was the one that didn't know what I was doing. I was the one who had screwed up. I'd been late, and now everything spun out of control.

Nylah walked to me. She took my hand and led me to a spot in the shade. She handed me a water bottle, and I drank.

"Maybe this was a mistake," I said, wiping my mouth with my sleeve. "Maybe I should have gone back home. Who am I kidding, trying to be something I'm not?"

Nylah studied my face. "Everything happens for a reason, Ellie."

"Yeah, a reason no one seems to understand. Not even you, who talks to the Goddess yourself. Seems like I'm not the only one that needs to try harder." I was snappy. I knew it and couldn't help myself. My frustration had a life of its own.

Nylah regarded me, her face closed. Another one of those masks everyone wore. She held out her hand. "Let me help you."

"Why?"

"You can fight me, Ellie, or you can let me help you." Her voice was hard, her eyes fiery, and her power swirled close to the surface.

I didn't want to comply, but I'd already disappointed Dex. If I drove Nylah away, too, I wouldn't get my answers.

I took her hand. Nylah closed her eyes, and her magic hummed. It sighed against my skin, and, like tendrils of fog, it penetrated my frustration and anger and slowly dissolved it. When it was done, I took a deep breath and let it out, and I saw clearer.

"I'm sorry," I said.

Nylah shook her head. "Don't be sorry. You're still new. You'll learn. If you don't give up, you'll get where you need to be."

I nodded. She was right.

The King appeared from a side door, and I stiffened. He was handsome as ever, with his dark hair and icy eyes, tall and powerful and commanding. I shivered. I looked awful. I was sweaty, and my hair was a mess. Then again, he'd seen me look worse. Not that it mattered either way. He was Fae. He was engaged. And his face was solemn.

My stomach turned. Was he here to reprimand me for being late? I was sure Dex had gone straight to him to tell him how terrible I was. He was here to tell me I wasn't fit to be a warrior; I was sure of it.

"How are things going?" he asked.

"Good," Nylah said with a smile. "We're working on countering magic."

The King nodded. "It's the basics of being a warrior. Dex tells me you trained hard yesterday."

I nodded, waiting for the axe to drop, but he said nothing else.

"It's going to take a bit of time for me to get fit and strong," I said when I wasn't being admonished. "But I promise I'll work hard."

"I'd expect nothing less," King Rainier said.

"Ren," Nylah said, standing. "Can I talk to you for a second?"

The King nodded, and they stepped out of earshot. I watched them as they talked. They didn't look like a king and his subject. They looked like friends. Siblings. She was playful with him, teasing him by the looks of things, and he humored her. They had a close relationship, that much was clear.

The door to the palace opened yet again, and Lucia stepped out. Didn't she let him do anything alone? When the King appeared somewhere, it was a matter of minutes before Lucia followed.

I watched as the King stiffened, his demeanor changing. Nylah changed, too. She took a step back from the King, and their laughter and easy relationship disappeared. Lucia glanced at me over the King's shoulder before she looked away. I wasn't even worth her time.

Finally, the King and future queen left, and Nylah turned back to me.

"You're different around the King," I pointed out.

"Different from what?"

I thought about it. "You're less tense. You smile more. And...you call him Ren."

Nylah nodded. "Ren and I grew up together. He's not just my king, he's like a brother to me, and my dearest friend. We've been through a lot together."

I ached at the thought of having such a close relationship with someone. I wished I'd had someone like that. My life had been lonely. I had trusted no one, turned to no one. Everything I'd been through, I'd been through alone.

I thought about Lucia coming in.

"Not when the future queen is around," I added. "Then you're both very stiff. Even the King, when they're engaged to be married."

Nylah nodded. "Lucia and Ren still have a lot to learn about each other. They're not comfortable around each other yet. Ruling together doesn't require a loving relationship. It requires teamwork."

I frowned. "They're not in a loving relationship?"

"Not yet," Nylah said. "The marriage isn't for love. The point is to create a strong bond, so they can rule together, moving in the same realm. They need to do what's good for the kingdom. It takes time to get used to each other."

"That doesn't seem right," I said.

She laughed. "No, but royal families don't have the luxury of marrying for love. It's about staying in the First Realm, and that takes careful planning. The royal family can't afford to move away from Terra, to be unable to rule with the power that she bestows upon them when they're where they belong."

It all seemed backward to me. "Isn't love supposed to be stronger than that?" I asked. "Love conquers all, right?"

Her laughter still danced in her eyes. "It would be nice to think so," she said. "But love is never enough, Ellie. If the King marries for love, but the bond isn't right, and it yanks him from Terra, he'll lose his power and his ability to reign the way he does. He can't afford to love before all else. If he finds love, that's a bonus."

"That's sad," I said.

Nylah nodded. "It is. But being in line to the throne has never been something anyone got excited about. It's hard work. It requires sacrifice. We all have to give something up if we want to make a difference."

I thought about that. Had I ever given up something important? Probably not. I'd had nothing to begin with.

"So, he could marry someone but never find love? Isn't that a requirement to make it work?" I asked. I had had little of an example of what love was supposed to be like—for that, I would have had to have a family. I'd read books, though. I was familiar with the concept.

"I know it's hard to understand," Nylah said. "Just be glad that the burden doesn't fall on you to make choices for the greater good, rather than for yourself."

I nodded.

"We should get back to training. How are you feeling? Ready to try again?"

I was in control now. I was in a better headspace. I nodded and stood.

Nylah and I walked to the center of the arena, and she started her magic again. This time, I knew what I was doing.

10

"How are you settling in?" Nylah asked when I joined her in the cathedral after my training sessions with Dex.

"I'm managing," I said. "I don't feel like a complete outsider anymore."

"Good. I hoped you would start feeling at home."

"I'm still human," I pointed out. This would never truly be my home.

"That's true. But that's not all you are. Will you bring me those scrolls?" She pointed at a pile of scrolls on her desk. I collected them in my arms and brought them to the coffee table. Nylah sat on the couch and shifted closer when the thick scrolls clattered onto the surface.

"If I'm not fully human, what am I?" I asked.

"For one, you're a victim of a spell, and that's not a coincidence."

"You keep saying that."

Nylah glanced at me. "And for another, you broke the gagging spell and shifted back into your own body. Humans can't do that."

"So..." I didn't know what that meant.

"Tell me about you, Ellie." She reached for one scroll, undid it, and opened it carefully so the paper would stay intact because the scrolls were old.

The change of topic was abrupt. "What do you mean, like my dreams?"

"What do you wish for? What do you hope to be one day?"

I shrugged. "We don't get to choose where we're headed or what we'll be. If we're lucky, we get to live."

Nylah pursed her lips. "I've never agreed with slavery or the way some Fae treat humans."

"There are rumors things will change."

"Ren will do what he can, but he can't change the way of the Fae overnight."

I didn't respond to that.

"I always wanted more," I said. "I fought my whole life—to stay alive, to survive, and to stay safe. That's all I've ever done, and after twenty-one years of fighting...I'm tired. I don't have *dreams,* per se. I just know that there must be a life where fighting isn't everything."

"And now you've chosen to fight yet again," Nylah said.

I shrugged. The irony wasn't lost on me. So much had changed. So many things were better.

"If everything is done with holotechnology, why do you still have these old scrolls? It seems like a waste of space." I looked at the shelves, filled with old books and scrolls that could fit onto a small holodevice Nylah could keep in a drawer.

"Magic. We can't transfer that to holodevices."

"What?"

"Here." She held out the scroll to me. I hesitated, unsure, before I touched it. When I did, whispers shivered around me, speaking of things I didn't understand. The words on the scroll came to life.

I jerked my hand back.

"What are we fighting for?" I asked, shifting uneasily on the couch. Nylah removed the scroll, and I let out a breath I didn't know I was holding. "We're training so hard, and I'm supposed to be part of this elite guard. But what for?"

"Change, Ellie," Nylah said. "We're fighting to undo the wrongs of the past."

"That's not possible," I said. "How are you supposed to change the past?"

"By not repeating it. Ren isn't his father, but it's so easy to follow the path already carved out. If he wants to veer from that path, he needs to fight to carve out a new one."

It sounded like a Fae problem. It had nothing to do with me. Except that I was a part of his elite guard now, so I guess it had everything to do with me.

"Why does magic scare you?" she asked.

"It doesn't," I said defiantly, jutting my chin into the air.

"Do you have a family?" Nylah asked.

I stilled. Dex had asked me that, too.

"No," I said tightly.

"No one at all?"

I shook my head. "They didn't want me."

Nylah's expression changed. Her eyes filled with sadness. "I'm sure that's not true."

"I'm not the orphan that believes I just got lost, and my mom is still out there, looking for me. That kind of hope kills. I know who I am, and I don't need them. I've gotten this far without help, and I'm doing just fine."

"You are," Nylah said. "But it never hurts to have someone in your corner. I'm in your corner, and so are Dex and the King."

When she mentioned King Rainier being in my corner, my chest tightened a little, and my heart fluttered. He wouldn't be in my corner like that, I reminded myself. He believed I would be an asset, and that was why I was here—not because he saw anything else in me.

I went weak at the knees whenever I saw him, but those feelings were one-sided.

"Would you like to come to me after training more often?" Nylah asked.

"Why?"

She looked at me, and it didn't offend her that I'd asked.

"Your company is pleasant. I'm always alone."

I didn't have a good reason to say no. So, I agreed. I enjoyed hanging out with her, too, not that I would admit to that.

I could be friends with Nylah, and that was rare. I'd never had a true friend.

⚜

WHERE MY RELATIONSHIP WITH NYLAH WAS GOING BETTER, DEX hadn't seemed to forget that I'd been late before.

He was still hard on me, even though I'd been on time this morning and for the past six days. He ran me through drills even harder than the days before. I had to run for miles, combined with strength training, only to run again.

By the time training was over, my lungs burned, and my legs screamed at me. Every muscle group was numb, and with every step I took, I feared I was going to fall over. Despite how hard I worked and how much I put my body through, I felt good. Stronger.

For the first time, I had a purpose.

"You can have a drink of water," Dex said, and I all but fell into the well next to the training arena when I went to fill my water bottle.

When I returned to the arena, my clothes soaked with the water I'd poured on myself and my hair, it wasn't Dex who stood there waiting for me.

It was King Rainier.

I swallowed hard. "Your Highness."

"Ellie." He nodded curtly. "I came to see how you were doing."

"I think I'm doing okay," I said. "But you'll have to ask Dex if he agrees."

I wiped my brow with my sleeve, feeling stupid for dumping all that water over me. I looked terrible, once again. I wanted the King to see a better side of me, but our meetings only happened when I looked disheveled.

"I did," King Rainier said. "He's pleased with your progress in such a short time. Nylah tells me you're an outstanding student, too."

Relief washed over me. "I didn't think it would show so soon. I'm in way over my head."

The King smiled, and his eyes were gentle.

"It takes time, but you have the potential. If you believe in yourself, it will be a killer combination to unlock something truly powerful."

I blinked at him. "That's very kind of you to say."

The King lifted his hand to my face and carefully brushed strands of wet hair from my cheek. He'd combed back his black hair. It accentuated his features—high cheekbones, a straight nose, and those blue eyes that bore into my soul.

When his fingertips touched my skin, warmth blossomed there. It translated into heat, rushing through my body.

My breath caught in my throat, and I looked into King Rainier's icy eyes. They seemed to melt, turning darker. Not the color of a glacier, but the color of the ocean it ran into.

The atmosphere shifted between us, and tension lay beneath the surface, thick and wanting. I leaned toward the King without knowing what I was doing.

He cleared his throat, and I snapped out of the spell. I stepped back.

"Well done," he said and clasped his hands behind his back. "At this rate, you might join the war."

War? Is Jasfin going to war? I wanted to ask, but I kept the question to myself.

I felt how closed off he was, where a moment ago he'd been wide open so that whatever had passed between us had happened without a thought. Now, reaching him was impossible.

"I have business to attend to," he said and turned away from me. "After lunch, Nylah will expect you." He spoke as he walked away, his words blowing away in the breeze that had picked up.

I stood in the arena, my head spinning. My skin still hummed where he'd touched me.

LUNCH CONSISTED OF FRESHLY BAKED BREAD, COLD CUTS OF MEAT, thick butter, and soup to go with it. I'd heard from the warriors that we ate like peasants, but to me, the food was fit for a king. The meals at the tavern were mediocre at best. The food made for the elite guard was better than anything I'd ever tasted.

Once I'd eaten my fill, showered, and dressed in a dress rather than training leathers, I made my way to the cathedral. Nylah was at her desk, scribbling with a furrowed brow.

When I walked in, she looked up and replaced her frustration with a smile.

"There you are. I have something I want you to look at."

She walked to the bookcase and grabbed a thick book, leather-bound with yellow pages that looked centuries old.

"What is it?"

"It's a history book," she said. She walked to the couches and sat down, gesturing for me to do the same. I collapsed onto the couch with a groan. My muscles ached after training. "I figured if you're going to fight with us, it will help if you know what you're fighting for."

She handed me the thick book. I sat up and took it from her. It was heavy, and my aching muscles complained when I hoisted it onto my lap.

I paged through the book. It was all handwritten, with maps drawn and descriptions explaining the lay of the land and how the countries had come to be.

"Speaking of fighting..." I closed the book and looked at Nylah. "The King came to see me after training."

"He's pleased," she said.

I nodded. "I hope so. But he mentioned being ready to fight in the war. What was he talking about?"

Nylah sighed. "War is a waste of time and resources, if you ask me. It sacrifices innocent lives for power control. War would never take place if everyone had the mind to sit down and be reasonable."

I waited for her to work through her thought process.

"You'll read about the countries in there," she said, gesturing to the book. "But I'm sure you know about the tension between the three countries: Jasfin, Palgia, and Tholand."

I nodded. I'd seen some maps, although I'd never really been taught anything formally.

"Jasfin and Palgia are on the brink of war."

"Why?"

"Resources," Nylah said with an easy shrug. "Falx, the King of Palgia, also known as the King of Darkness, is greedy. He's ruined his own country and stripped it of all that represents life. Now, he wants what we have. For centuries, Jasfin has been more powerful, but Palgia is catching up."

"How?"

"King Falx is a Conjurite. He uses dark magic to enforce his evil and reign in terror."

I shook my head, frowning. "What's a Conjurite?"

Nylah closed her eyes, and it looked like what she told me pained her.

"We draw our power from the Goddess Terra. Fae get their magic from her, where they walk in the Neutral Realm. But the Conjurites don't draw their power from Terra. They draw it from darkness. It's a terrible magic, and it kills what it touches. Maybe not right away, but slowly. It's why Palgia is slowly dying, and there is nothing left of the beauty that once was."

Jasfin was incredibly beautiful. Lush forests, rolling fields, corn-flower blue skies and thunderstorms that made every living being tremble. Steepholde, where I'd grown up, was a village close to the southern coastline, and the mild climate made it an ideal place to live.

Even here, near the palace and the mountains, the forests were lush, and the Fae lived in cottages between the trees.

I tried to envision what the view from King Rainier's window must have been like if everything had been dead and the river dried up.

"It sounds awful," I said. "Where does this dark magic come from?"

"I don't know," Nylah admitted. "I've asked Terra, but she won't show me anything. I've done all the reading I could, combing through tomes and scrolls and every book I could get my hands on. Fae have to give up the light—the magic we use—to use Conjurite magic. In Jasfin, many do this to survive because so much darkness surrounds them."

"Why?"

She shrugged. "For the sake of being powerful."

I shook my head. I was learning so much about the world I lived in, things I'd never known before. I'd grown up around Fae and served them, but I'd known nothing other than my need to survive, keeping my nose clean, and steering clear of magic if it would kill me.

"Ren has more power than the kings of the past," Nylah said. "We look to him to save us. If anyone can lead us through this war, it will be him."

"That's a lot of pressure," I said, thinking about what Dex had said to me about the King.

"It is. And war is devastating. If we stand together, and Ren stands firm on what he believes, there's hope yet."

I nodded. Hope was all we really had.

The conversation changed from the war to Nylah's life growing up. Nylah told me more about how she'd grown up in the palace with Ren, studying here in the cathedral, and playing with him when she took a break.

I smiled sadly.

"What's wrong?" Nylah asked.

"I know it sounds silly," I said. "But when you talk about your friendship with the King, and I see how Dex is with him…I wish I had people like that in my life growing up. I had no one. I lived in an orphanage, and I hadn't seen my adoptive family since I was sixteen. Any kids I met were just as broken as I was. Playing wasn't something we had time to do between cleaning, cooking, or working to bring in money for the orphanage. After that, it was all about working, so I could survive on my own."

Nylah shook her head. "I'm horrified at how you grew up."

I chuckled, not because my story was funny, but because I was uncomfortable being so vulnerable. "It didn't bother me before. Only now, when I see the stark contrast between this life and the one I used to have."

"Well, you're here now," Nylah said warmly. She put her hand on my arm, and warmth and magic pulsed there. "And you have us to lean on and to turn to. We may not have known each other for centuries, the way Ren and I have—"

"Centuries?"

Nylah's eyes glittered. "Ren and I are both five hundred years old."

I gasped. I knew the Fae grew much older than humans, but five *hundred?*

"I'm twenty-one," I said meekly.

She smiled. "It doesn't matter how many years you have. It matters what you do with them. Some Fae can live a millennium and have nothing to show for it."

I blinked at her. A millennium? Really?

"What I mean to say," Nylah went on, picking up where I'd interrupted her. "Ren and I spent a lot of time together over the years, but that doesn't mean it's what it takes to forge a friendship. You have a friend in me, Ellie."

"You see me as a friend?" I asked, surprised.

She nodded. "Of course."

I already felt more welcome and wanted than anywhere else in my life, no matter how long I'd been there.

Was it crazy to see this place as home?

⚘ 11 ⚘

It was a week later when I stepped into the arena, and I expected to see Nylah. She had been training me in the mornings along with Dex.

Instead of Nylah meeting me, King Rainier stood in the arena, upright and proud. He wore training leather, much like what Dex usually wore, but golden thread created an intricate embroidered design on his chest and sleeves. His dark hair, usually neat, was messy, as if he'd spent his time pushing his hands into it. I wanted to touch it, to push my hands into it, too, to see what it felt like.

"Your Highness," I said with an awkward curtsy. He smirked when I did, and I felt silly. "Is everything okay?"

He nodded. "Perfectly fine. Nylah had to take care of business, so I'm going to train you for the day."

I stared at him. The *King* was going to train me?

"Don't look so shocked," he said. "I was here once, too, you know. Dex and I trained side by side."

Of course, that had been centuries ago, but that was true. I had to remember that despite being a powerful ruler, he must have started somewhere. Although, he had magic, so he would always be more powerful than me.

"Let's get to training," he said.

Without warning, he spun around and threw magic my way. It came out of the blue, but I did what Nylah had taught me. I sank into my center, turning my focus inward.

King Rainier's power was much stronger than what Nylah had been using on me, and fighting it wasn't easy. But I did it—the power bounced off me after fighting to get through my block.

When I looked up, the King looked impressed.

"You're stronger than you look."

"I've been practicing."

I did what Nylah had suggested. Every night before bed, I meditated and practiced focusing, finding my center, and keeping my focus there, even when I had my eyes open and did other things. Like brushing my hair or my teeth.

The King attacked again. This time, the power was almost too much to handle. I deflected it, but he attacked at the same time. He spun around, lifting his leg to place a kick in my gut. I blocked that, although it was clumsy. When he hit me, I blocked the blow and countered.

He was holding back. He had a lot more in him, but I was proud of what I'd done. This was the first time I'd had to face magic and physical attacks at once. I'd worked on blocking magic with Nylah and fighting with Dex, but never together.

"You're getting there," the King said, nodding. "I'm pleased."

"Thank you." I beamed, pleased with myself.

The King attacked again, and again, and again. It turned out he was a tougher trainer than Dex. He was hard on me, insisting I push myself harder, faster.

And the King was more powerful and more alpha than Dex could ever be. It was because he was king, I was sure, but he knew who he was and what he was capable of. He was upright and tall, and his confidence oozed out of him. It was intimidating.

It wasn't only his attitude that was a challenge to come up against. Physically, the King was like a god. Muscular, powerful, both with magic and physical strength. But his size wasn't a disadvantage. I thought I had speed on my side because I wasn't as tall and strong as he was. The King, however, was agile as hell, and I couldn't get around him.

We fought with him training me as we worked. His voice was sharp, his words clipped as he barked out commands. I did my best, fighting as hard as I could, giving it my all, but he demanded more.

"You're going to face warriors who won't let up because you're getting tired," he said. "When we train, we don't train until we're tired, we train until we're down. And out there, we don't fight until we feel it's enough. We fight until we win. Or die."

His words were hard to hear. He was right, obviously. War wasn't an easy thing to prepare for, but King Rainier seemed to have no mercy, and he pushed me harder and further, still.

Finally, when I couldn't breathe anymore and my muscles trembled when I so much as thought about moving, the King nodded and stepped back.

I needed the break. My lungs burned with every inhale.

I turned to pick up my water bottle, and just then, the King attacked another time. I wasn't ready, and a blow against the head had me sprawling on the ground.

"Watch your back at all times. The enemy won't wait for you to face them before they attack."

I lay on the ground, gasping for air. I felt like my body was going to implode. I couldn't breathe.

"Ellie?" King Rainier asked. "Oh, Goddess."

He hurried to me where I lay on the floor, mouth opening and closing like a fish. He turned me onto my back and pulled up my arms, so they were above my head. My chest opened, my diaphragm did what it was supposed to, and air filled my lungs again.

I gasped, sucking in mouthfuls of air, relearning how to breathe.

"Are you okay?" he asked with concern in his voice. His thick brows knitted together, his eyes widened.

I pushed up, nodding, and suddenly, our faces were only inches from each other. Our eyes locked, and his eyes were drowning deep, filled with worry and an expression I struggled to decipher. His warm breath caressed my skin, and I clenched my fists to stop myself from reaching out to run my finger along his jawline...and his lips.

His eyes slid to my mouth for just a moment. We were caught in a bubble, and time stood still as he stared at me. I wondered what it would feel like if he pressed his lips against mine. Emotions flowed between us without a barrier, and it was inviting and comfortable. My core tightened, anticipating what would come next.

He moved so close, our lips nearly brushed together. If I moved only a fraction, we would touch, but I was frozen in his arms, staring into the depths of his eyes, feeling like I could drown in them.

He cleared his throat and pulled back, and it broke the spell. He stood and offered me a hand, pulling me to my feet. Whatever had flowed between us a moment ago was gone. He'd shut that door again, and we were only two warriors, standing together.

"Well done, Ellie," Rainier said curtly. "You've trained hard today, and I'm pleased with your progress." He glanced at the time. "I have meetings to attend. You're dismissed."

The formality in his tone was jarring after he'd been so warm and open toward me. I nodded and waited for him to walk away before I turned and headed toward the warrior quarters.

My head spun.

He'd almost kissed me. He hadn't done it, but he'd thought about it. That didn't make sense.

I'd started to understand how Fae relationships worked. I'd been reading the books Nylah gave me every time I saw her—some on the history of the land, and some on the Fae so that I could better understand the life I was to live here among them. The Fae created bonds, and when two Fae bonded, they didn't have eyes for anyone else.

The way Rainier had looked at me had been wrong. He was bonded to Lucia, wasn't he? Or were the legends wrong?

"My lady," Bessie greeted when I walked into the room.

I just wanted to be alone. I needed time to think about what had happened.

"I'll take care of myself for now, Bessie," I said.

She frowned. "Are you all right?"

"Is it wrong to want to be alone?"

She shook her head. "You seem...distressed."

I sighed. "It was a hard training session. The King trained me, and it was..." My cheeks flushed when I thought about him, his powerful hands on my body when he'd helped me up.

Bessie's eyes twinkled. "He's quite something, isn't he?"

I blushed harder. "I'd like to take a bath."

"I'll draw one for you," she said.

The corners of her mouth twitched with a smile. I hated that she'd seen me blushing about the King. But it was Bessie—she was always here, and I saw her as a friend of sorts. She knew what happened behind the scenes. And I could relate to her because she was a human servant. That's all I had ever been until King Rainier offered me a position as a warrior.

When Bessie announced the bath was ready, I thanked her, and she left without me needing to dismiss her a second time. I stripped off my clothes and dumped them into the laundry basket before I climbed into the hot water. The tub was filled to the brim, and the water was up to my chin. I added bath salts and foam to ease the ache in my muscles.

When I lay back in the bath, I closed my eyes. I'd fallen asleep here more than once, drained after training.

But today, my thoughts kept wandering to Rainier and the way he'd looked at me. I'd wanted him to kiss me. I wanted to know what it would be like to have his lips on mine, and his large body pressed up against me. His hands roaming my body...

I slid my hands over my body under the water, my skin slippery with the bath salts and minerals. Heat washed through my body, and I touched myself, cupping my breasts. My nipples were erect with lust, and my center throbbed and ached with need.

It was wrong of me to think about the King this way. It was wrong of me to want a male who belonged to another. But the way he'd looked at me, with eyes filled with a desire that echoed my own... My imagination took over.

I imagined my hands were his and slid them over my curves. I pushed my fingers into the folds of my sex and ran them in circles over my clit. I imagined it was his tongue pleasuring me.

The lust unfurled at my core and spread through my body, and I rubbed myself faster and faster. I gasped, and the water lapped up and splashed against the side of the tub, dripping on the floor. But my eyes were closed, and I pictured the King, his body naked and hovering over mine. He was so tall and broad to my slight figure. He could crush me with his strength, but the gentleness I'd seen in his eyes had told me he wouldn't hurt me. The concern when he'd thought he *had* hurt me told me I was safe.

I pictured him rearing over me as his thick cock plunged into me, taking everything I wanted to give him.

When the orgasm took over my body, I cried out, my body jerking and contracting as pleasure washed over me in waves.

It took only a moment before the orgasm faded, but I breathed hard, muscles trembling. I submerged myself in the hot water and relished in the aftermath of my pleasure, letting the thoughts of being with the King linger just a bit longer before I would have to force them away again.

I didn't see the King for a week after that. At first, I hoped he would come to train me again. I wanted to see him, to get to know him. I wanted to see if the same connection, the same spark, would appear. Or had it only been a one-off thing?

But he stayed away.

Was it because of what had happened? Or was it because he was busy doing his duties and taking care of business? I hoped it was the latter, but I worried it was the former.

When I arrived in the arena one morning, it wasn't Nylah who was there to meet me, the way she usually was. It wasn't King Rainier, either.

Lucia awaited me.

"Hello, Ellie," she said sweetly.

"Your Highness," I said politely.

"Oh, none of that," she laughed. The sound rubbed against my skin like sandpaper, and I cringed. "When we're training, we're equals. You can call me Lucia."

"You're training me today?" I asked, unsure. I glanced at her clothing.

Lucia wore what could pass for training clothes, if it hadn't been so embellished with diamonds and thread. Her pants and top were leather, as were mine, but hers looked like they were more for show. Her long blonde hair hung loose over her shoulders, too. She hadn't tied it back and out of the way for a training session.

"Nylah is busy," Lucia said. "*Everyone* is busy." By the way she emphasized the word, I assumed she meant Rainier, too. "I offered to step in and help. I like to meet with the female warriors from time to time, you know. Us girls need to stick together." Her smile was syrupy sweet, and she winked at me.

"Okay," I said.

Lucia nodded, and without warning, she threw a wave of magic at me. It was scalding hot, like metal in the fire, and I had to concentrate on fighting it. I blocked it, because I'd learned how to focus on my center immediately, and the magic bounced off me. The heat lingered on my skin, and I shook my hands, trying to get rid of the pain. She'd physically burned me.

I shook it off—damned if I let on how much it hurt.

"You've been working hard," Lucia said, circling me.

We were supposed to be working together, but I got the feeling she was circling me the way a predator did its prey.

"I'm trying my best," I said.

I turned with her, facing her at all times. If I gave her my back, she would catch me off guard.

She wasn't my friend, even though she was trying to make it seem like she was. I was wary of her.

"Let's do another one," she said.

She threw more magic at me. This time, it was more powerful, and it was hard to block. Heat danced on my skin, and I let out a yelp that made her smirk with satisfaction. She wanted me to hurt, but I blocked it. I was stronger, healthier, and I'd found that my physical strength made a difference to how well I could focus and deflect magic.

Lucia narrowed her eyes. I wasn't buckling the way she wanted me to.

"Do you think King Rainier let you train here because you're a good fighter?"

"That's what he said."

"He let you stay because he pities you. You're nothing but a pest, but he has a soft heart—too soft."

"That's how you talk of the male you're going to marry?"

"We should understand each other's strengths and weaknesses."

"So far, the only weakness I can see in the King...is you."

She glared at me. "I see what you're doing, you know." Her voice was crisp now, sharp on my skin when she spoke.

"What?" I asked.

"You're trying to worm your way into a position of power."

She threw power at me. It burned on my skin, a searing heat like I'd stood too close to the flame. I deflected again. The blow was hard enough that I staggered back, although I kept my footing.

"I don't know what you mean," I said. "I was offered a position as a warrior. I didn't ask for it."

"No, but you could have turned it down. You didn't."

"I wasn't going to go back to the squalor I used to live in."

Lucia glanced at me down her nose. "That, my dear, would have been the best thing for you to do. You don't belong here."

"I'm grateful for the opportunity to train here and fight in the name of the King."

Lucia laughed, and I wanted to rub my arms to get rid of the awful sensation that came with it. It was like her laughter was laced with power. I fought the urge to spit out the bad taste it left in my mouth.

"Let me explain something to you, little *human*," she said, coming closer to me. She was taller than I was, and she looked down at me like I was disgusting, a scowl on her face. "I know you think you belong here, but you don't. You're nothing more than a slave."

The humans were often slaves to the Fae. For centuries, the Fae had used humans, but there were those who were born free, and we were a growing breed.

"I'm a free woman."

"Yes, you are. For now," Lucia said. "But if you try to wriggle your way into the palace, you won't get very far. You should know your place."

Before I could clap back, she shoved her power at me, and this time, she wasn't holding back. I slammed into the ground, crying out as the magic filled me, scalding. Flames engulfed me. Lucia's hands didn't touch me, they only hovered above my chest, but her power crushed me. Her magic filled me up like a cup of boiling water and threatened to pull me apart at the seams from the inside.

I cried out and tried to turn my attention inward—to focus the way Nylah had taught me to do. The future Fae queen's power was too strong, though, and the pain was crippling. I couldn't think straight.

Lucia's face was just above mine, and her face was twisted into a snarl. Her blue eyes darkened and narrowed, and her blonde hair whipped around wildly from her power. She looked more like a demon than the image of beauty. The edges of my vision blurred, and fear took hold in the pit of my stomach. This was it. She was going to kill me.

This was where I was going to die.

"Stop!" I was vaguely aware of a voice calling from the side. A familiar voice.

My vision darkened completely, and my blood rushed in my ears. My heart hammered against my chest, beating too fast. It was going to burst if Lucia didn't stop. But she wouldn't stop, would she?

A second wave of magic came from the side like a wave, and it physically threw Lucia off me. She cried out as she tumbled to the side.

The wave of magic washed over me, calming and soothing like water, and I had the strangest illusion of the ocean, washing waves onto the shore.

My vision slowly returned.

"What the hell do you think you're doing?" Nylah cried out. "If you so much as lay another hand or a drop of magic on Ellie, I will see to it you're not *fit* to be queen."

Her power pulsed to where I lay in the dust, and it was laced with fury. She was so angry, and I felt the heat on my skin like that of a furnace. She was much more powerful than Lucia. She moved in the Second Realm, and Lucia only in the first—or she would one day, but Lucia wasn't royal yet.

I watched Nylah storm across the arena to where Lucia pushed herself up from the dirt. She dusted herself off.

"Do you have any idea who I am?" Lucia spat. "This will go straight to the King. How dare you threaten me, your future queen?"

"If I didn't come here, Goddess knows what you would have done!" Nylah cried.

"And look at what you *did*," Lucia said. Her voice was calm now. "The King will hear about your insubordination. Don't think that your friendship with him will save you once I'm through telling him how you—"

"I'll tell him how you tried to kill Ellie," Nylah said hotly. "If you lose your place as queen, it's nobody's fault but your own."

Lucia clenched her jaw, and her eyes spewed fire, but she didn't clap back.

"This isn't the end of it, High Priestess," she said coolly.

"I imagine it's not," Nylah replied.

Lucia walked away, her blonde hair flowing behind her, wafting in the breeze. Aside from the dust on her leather clothes, she looked like she could have stepped from the screen of a holo-magazine.

Nylah rushed to me, where I tried to push myself up. My whole body ached, and my head spun when I tried to move.

"Are you okay?" she asked, falling to her knees at my side.

I fell back, unable to sit. The pain was intense.

"I don't think I can move," I admitted. I squeezed my eyes shut, and tears threatened to spill onto my cheeks. If I couldn't fight, I couldn't stay. What if Lucia had done too much damage?

"I've got you," Nylah said.

With the help of her magic, she got me up. She draped my arm across her shoulders and wrapped an arm around my waist, using her magic to get me to walk.

She helped me to the cathedral and into a large room I'd never been in. When she laid me on the bed, I spotted pictures on the mantle and realized this was Nylah's room.

"I'm sorry," I mumbled.

"Don't be," she told me. She stroked my hair, her voice soothing. "You did nothing wrong. If I hadn't come to check on you, who knows what she would have done." She shuddered before she closed her eyes. "Just drink it in. Let the magic do its job, okay?"

I was too tired to nod. Nylah closed her eyes and hovered her hands over my body, and I did what she said. I let the magic wash over me, drinking it in. Nylah rebuilt me, undoing the damage that had been done.

She saved me, pulling me back from the edge.

I didn't know how long I'd been in her room, but by the time I was strong enough to be moved—not nearly strong enough to walk on my own—servants took me back to my room, where I fell into a deep, dreamless slumber.

❦ 13 ❦

I drifted in and out of sleep. It felt like I had a heavy weight around my ankles, and it kept pulling me underwater so that I couldn't breathe. When my lungs were on the verge of bursting and I was about to drown, I would resurface again, gasping for air.

I lost count of how many times it happened. I lost track of time. All I knew was that I was in my bed, and that it was dark outside.

Lucia had tried to kill me—the bitch—and Nylah had saved my life.

Servants came and went—Bessie and others—refilling water pitchers I couldn't remember drinking from, checking my temperature in case Nylah had to come for me again. But she didn't come.

That had to be a good thing. I was in my own room. I couldn't remember when it had happened, but it meant I had to be out of danger if I wasn't in the High Priestesses' bed anymore.

When I slept—when it didn't feel like I was drowning, and I could just rest—I dreamed. I wasn't sure of what—of people I didn't know, of places I'd never seen before. In one dream, I was surrounded by light and by people who loved me, but in a separate dream, King Rainier was there.

He was standing on the horizon, waving, calling my name. I wanted to answer, but my voice was gone, or the wind blew my words away before they reached him.

"Ellie," I heard him. "Ellie."

"I can't reach you," I said.

"Ellie, you're dreaming."

I blinked my eyes open, and I was in my room once more. Bessie had piled blankets high on my bed, but I was shivering.

Rainier sat on the edge of my bed, his face riddled with concern.

"Your Highness," I croaked, fully awake now.

I tried to sit up, but he shook his head.

"Don't get up. Please. Just rest."

I sank back onto my pillows. Rainier reached for a glass of water and handed it to me. When I pressed it to my lips, the water was soothing. My skin was scorching hot.

"Do I have a fever?" I asked.

Rainier nodded. "It's your body, trying to fight the magic."

"Will it last long?"

"Not too much longer. Nylah's magic is fighting it. You have a fever because there is a war raging within you."

"Feels about right," I said.

Rainier smiled sadly at that. "I'm sorry."

"For what?"

"For Lucia and what she did to you—for her behavior, overall. Sometimes, she doesn't know her limits."

I stared at Rainier. "She did it intentionally."

He sighed. "She's being dealt with. I won't allow her to do anything like that again."

"How can you control her?" I asked. "What stops her from doing it again?"

"She won't. I talked to her. And she..." Rainier frowned. He seemed to have lost track of what he'd wanted to say—or of what had happened.

"What did she say to you?" I asked.

"She said she was sorry," Rainier said.

'Sorry' didn't cut it. 'Sorry' wasn't enough to undo that she'd tried to kill me. Why was everyone so calm about it? Because she was the future queen? Or was it something else? What if it was magic?

"Does everyone like her?" I asked.

"She has her flaws," the King admitted.

Understatement of the year.

"Lucia is a problem," I said.

Rainier raised his brows. "She's a little unsure of her role as the future queen, but she'll learn. We should all have the luxury of space to learn and grow."

"Her magic is wrong," I said.

Rainier put his hand on mine, and electricity jolted through me at the touch.

"You have a lot to learn, but you should watch your tongue. She is the future queen."

He removed his hand, and I felt his absence acutely. My mind spun.

He believed Lucia had just made a mistake. He was taking her side. She was doing this. She was controlling them somehow, making them believe she was in the right place.

How did she do it?

I wanted to challenge him, to counter him. I wanted to know what she was doing and how. But he wouldn't know if he was in the same boat as everyone else.

I turned my attention to the King. He seemed more open toward me, warmer, but not the way it had been between us in the arena when he'd trained me. It felt like an eternity ago now. He saw something in her. Had he seen something in me back then, too?

"How did you know Lucia was your mate?" I blurted out.

I colored when the words left my mouth, and Rainier looked surprised. He raised his eyebrows, lips parting.

"The way the Fae create bonds with their mates is foreign to me," I said.

Actually, love was foreign altogether, since I'd grown up mostly without it. I didn't tell him about my upbringing in the orphanage or the abusive family that eventually adopted me. Lucia's words stayed with me. I didn't want his pity.

Rainier shook his head. "Lucia isn't my mate."

I frowned. "I thought... Don't Fae mate?"

"They do," he said, nodding. "A mate bond is the strongest form of love. As Fae, we can get married without having a mate bond, like humans do. We still have the ability to love our partners, even without it. In fact, a mate bond is rarer than you might think. Most married Fae aren't mated."

"And you don't have that with her? The mate bond?"

He hesitated. I was asking him very personal questions, come to think of it.

"Our relationship is a political alliance. Lucia's family is very powerful." That was interesting. Exactly how powerful were they? "They have a lot of influence over the kingdom. In my position, I need to look at the bigger picture when I choose a bride."

I nodded. That part made sense. I saw what pressures he was under as a king. It didn't seem that his life belonged to him at all, but to the kingdom he served. It was backward. I would have thought, as king, he could do what he wanted. But it looked like the opposite was true— the more important he became, the less freedom he had. Ironically, it was almost like the slaves in the kingdom.

"I'm sorry about your father's death," I said instead.

Rainier looked surprised. "Thank you."

"It's been a bit of a wild ride since I arrived," I admitted. "I never got to tell you that. It was Conjurite magic that killed him, wasn't it? I read about it in something that Nylah made me read about the current political state of Jasfin."

His emotions opened like a floodgate. Sorrow flowed from him to me, so much of it—but bitterness, too, and betrayal. It went so much deeper than just saying, 'someone killed my father.'

"Did the Fae who killed your father—Zander—choose to be a Conjurite?"

"He wanted the power. He didn't care what he would lose to get it," Rainier said. "I want to find out who tried to pin the death on you by changing your appearance to look like him. I want to figure out what's going on. I'm sure if we find the Fae who hexed you, we'll know what happened."

Rainier had balled his hands into fists, and anger riddled his features. The heat of it was scalding hot on my skin, like a dry heat that singed everything in its path. As if he realized he was with me, he swallowed his fury and relaxed his hands. He pulled back and put himself back together again.

"What was your dad like?" I asked.

Rainier laughed bitterly, shaking his head. "He was a slave driver, actually. Hard on everyone, and he wanted things done the minute he thought of it. Patience wasn't his strong suit, and he could be a mean piece of work if he wanted to be. He was a good king, though. He cared about his citizens, even if it was in a twisted way. He understood sacrifice, even if he didn't understand where to draw the line. He gave everything for this kingdom, even at the expense of his family, sometimes..." Rainier swallowed. "He was a dick, to be honest." He laughed, a little embarrassed, before his laughter faded. "But still...he didn't deserve to die. I didn't want him gone, no matter how often we got stuck. He was all I had."

"Your mother..."

"She died during childbirth. They tell me she was an angel—not in the literal sense—but I didn't get the chance to see that. My father, with all his flaws, may he rest in peace, was the only family I had. Blood, anyway. Dex and Nylah are still here, of course, but that's different."

I nodded. I didn't know any of it. But judging by the way he felt about his father and his friends—what I *felt* radiating from him when he talked about them—he still had a lot of pain to process.

Rainier cleared his throat, and that strange sensation of knowing what he felt withdrew. He stood.

"I'll let you rest. I'm glad you're safe. Again, I apologize for my fiancée's actions. They were despicable, and I will make sure it's taken care of."

"Thank you," I said. I wasn't sure it would be that simple. I had a feeling something was wrong—*very* wrong, but I couldn't say it to anyone.

He nodded curtly before he left the room, leaving me alone.

I reached for the glass on the nightstand and took another sip of water before I lay back and closed my eyes.

Lucia wasn't Rainier's mate. It made me happy to know that. Someone like Rainier deserved more than that horrible female—a magical, conniving one at that.

However, they would still be married unless he found out who she truly was. There was nothing I could do about it until I could expose her. That would free him. It would remove her and allow him to be himself again. I was almost sure that she was using magic in a way that bound them all.

All but me.

But even if I could get rid of her, it wasn't like I could ever stand a chance with someone like Rainier. Besides the fact that he was the King, and I was just a peasant, he was the most powerful Fae that had ever lived. I was just a human. He could live for thousands of years, and I was doomed to less than a century.

Even if everything else somehow worked itself out, I would be nothing more than a drop in the ocean of his existence.

I closed my eyes and tried not to think anymore. My head hurt like hell, and thinking about never being good enough for Rainier caused my chest to ache, too.

14

It took another day or so for my body and Nylah's magic to fight against whatever Lucia had done to me. In two days, I was back in the arena, training with Dex and Nylah, following our usual routine. I trained harder. I couldn't afford for something to happen again. The Fae all around me were more powerful than I was, and I hated feeling like I was at the bottom of the food chain. I pushed myself to focus for longer, training by meditating. I asked Dex and Nylah to train me together, using magic and physical attacks so that I was on my toes, ready for anything.

After the third day back in the arena, I felt good. I sat on the floor, drinking water. Dex and Nylah stood to one side, talking about important business I couldn't hear. When I glanced toward the palace windows, I noticed Rainier watching me.

His eyes were on me—it was the reason I'd looked up at all.

His gaze shivered along my spine, cold and trembling, but heat came with it, too. It hypnotized me.

The atmosphere shifted. A breeze picked up and brought with it a sense of foreboding. I frowned and looked at Nylah and Dex. They were still deep in conversation, but Nylah cut herself short and looked around her.

She felt it as well.

"Dex—" she started.

The door to the warrior quarters crashed open, and Fae poured out through the door. Their faces twisted into snarls. They had weapons raised, and with a terrible warrior's cry, they ran toward us. Dex and Nylah stood frozen, and I gaped at what unfolded before me. I couldn't believe what I saw.

The first warriors reached Nylah. Dex jumped to the racks of equipment and grabbed a sword and a spear.

"Nylah!" he shouted and threw the sword toward her.

Nylah had her hand up, power flowing from her fingers that warded off the attackers. But they also had magic. They fought her barrier, and shockwaves of power came toward me as their magic clashed.

Nylah let them go, her sword raised. Magic exploded around her when she let out a cry and brought the sword down on the first warrior.

I couldn't keep watching. The attackers were on me now, too. I jumped up, and when magic hurtled toward me, I did what Nylah had taught me to do—I shifted my focus inward and fought it off.

"We're under attack!" someone shouted from the watchtower.

If only that warning would have come a few minutes sooner. Before he could shout again, an arrow pierced his chest, and the limp body fell from the tower.

My blood ran cold, and I had to think quick.

I ran to the equipment rack and found a sword and shield. It was heavy, but adrenaline strengthened me. The hand-to-hand combat came as second nature. I didn't have to think about blocking the strikes, twist out of the kicks, and return the blows. Dex had taught me well, building on the fighting skills I'd taught myself.

"Ellie!" Nylah screamed, and when I looked over my shoulder, a sword flew in my direction.

I twisted in the air, avoiding the blade, and lifted the shield so the sword clattered to the ground. The next warrior on me had a ball and chain, and I lifted the shield again, blocking the blow before I finished the warrior without a hitch.

They surrounded us.

It didn't take long before Rainier joined the fight. I didn't have time to see him with the attacks raining down on me, but it was poetry in motion to watch him in battle. He had fluid movements and a strength that was unparalleled.

The rest of the elite guard arrived, dressed for war, and their collective fury overpowered whatever else I might have felt. When the elite guard joined the fray, we were no longer overpowered. All around me, swords clanged, and screams created a backdrop for the arena.

"What have we got?" I heard Zita asking one warrior while she fought effortlessly. She made it look like a warmup.

"A bit of excitement, for a change," the warrior answered.

Zita laughed and finished off the attacker with ease.

"Ellie, watch out!" she yelled, and I spun around.

Another attacker came toward me with a large sledgehammer. I was painfully aware of their medieval weapons when everything around us seemed state-of-the art. It was almost primitive.

I wasn't strong enough to fight off the enormous man, and Rainier ran to me. He blocked the blow, and it was as if that gateway between us had opened again. We fought side by side, and I knew what he would do and when he would do it. Together, we took on a few more men. We moved in unison. I struck when he blocked and vice versa. When he ducked, I was there to fill in for him, and when he stood, I came from behind.

One by one, the bodies dropped. Fury and fear fueled me. Fury, coming from Rainier. It was searing hot, like a heatwave pressing down —and acrid fear, my own. But we succeeded. I fought off the clutching hands of terror that threatened to wrap around my throat and squeeze. I took deep breaths, ignoring that my breathing was getting harder. Ren had asked me to stay because I was a good fighter. So, I would be that fighter. The fear would not take hold of me. I wouldn't let it.

When the fight was over, bodies lay strewn around us on the training arena floor. Blood stained the sand. It was on my hands, splattered on my face and neck and smeared on my arms and legs.

The other warriors looked just as bad. Zita had smears of blood on her face, chest heaving, but she grinned white teeth. She lived for the fight.

I didn't feel elated at all.

My heart hammered against my chest, and my breath rasped in and out of my lungs as I gasped for air. My legs trembled, my knuckles were sore, and my fingers felt fused to the hilt of the sword.

Rainier and I locked eyes. His chest rose and fell in sync with my own breath. Sweat glistened on his brow. Was he aware of the connection?

I started trembling. The adrenaline faded, and I sank to the ground, unable to keep myself up anymore. I'd been detached, watching as if from afar. Now I crashed down to earth, and I was in the center of it all.

"Oh, no...no," I said, looking around.

There was so much blood, so much carnage, and so much *death*. And at my hands.

"It's okay, Ellie," Nylah said, coming to me. She looked just as dirty and splattered with blood as everyone else, but her eyes were steely, her expression solemn. "This was an act of war, and you did what you needed to do."

"How did they get into the palace?" Rainier boomed, turning toward the palace like a thunderstorm.

His ire crackled in the air, electricity around us. Everyone shied away from him and the power that spread away from him in waves.

A servant appeared, looking terrified.

"They posed as messengers, Your Highness," he said in a trembling voice. "Only a handful of them, with word from Palgia. When I allowed them in, they overran us with the rest of them coming through. The warriors were all locked up in their quarters until one servant could set them free. A few escaped through the windows."

"What? Locked up?"

"It seems to have been carefully planned, with an inside man, Your Highness," the servant said. "A thousand apologies."

Rainier shook his head. "They came for a reason." He looked at me. His eyes filled with emotion—fury because of the attack, but concern, too. They changed color, as they'd done before, going from glacial blue to cerulean in an instant. I felt him, his feelings, as I had many times before. He reached for me through a connection I now knew I wasn't imagining. It was the first time he actively responded to me through this invisible pull I had to him. As if he realized it, he shut it down again. He withdrew, and his anger rose to the surface again. It masked his concern. "And that is to take you out."

"Me?" My blood drained from my face, and my mouth ran dry. "How do you know?" I demanded.

"You were the person they came for. They knew exactly what they wanted and where they were headed."

I shook my head. "I wasn't the only one out here." I looked up at Nylah.

She nodded, and Dex looked grim. He clenched his jaw, and the murderous look on his face suggested he wished there were more of them to kill off.

"They're all dead," Rainier said, looking around him at the carnage we'd left behind. "Pity. I would have loved to question someone about what this was all about."

He scowled.

I started feeling lightheaded at the sight of all the blood. I'd fought a lot before, but I'd never killed. This was gruesome. Gruesome and somehow my fault.

"Come with me," Nylah said. Her voice was gentle but urgent, and she put her hand on my elbow. She helped me up and steered me out of the arena and away from the devastation we'd created. "You need to be healed," she said while we walked to the cathedral. "Let Ren and Dex take care of the aftermath."

I was happy to let her take me away. Did I need healing? I hadn't even felt the wounds on my arms and hands. They were only tiny nicks and cuts, but now that the adrenaline had faded, they stung and burned.

"We need tea," she told a servant who appeared when we walked into the cathedral. "Very sweet. She's in shock."

We sat on the couch in Nylah's living room. She asked another servant to bring her a tray with different salves and potions, and with magic and the aid of these pots and vials, she healed my wounds.

My mind kept spinning. I flashed on the dead bodies all around me, but the most prominent in my mind was the way Rainier and I had connected with each other.

"How do you fight when you're all in each other's heads?" I asked.

"What?"

"I can't even think straight when I'm alone in my head in a fight like that. To have someone else in there is exhausting."

Nylah stared at me. "What are you talking about?"

"Ren...feeling him when we fight. Knowing where he is and what he's going to do, so that we can all work together."

Nylah's expression looked more and more confused as I spoke.

"Doesn't everyone have that?" Until now, I'd thought it was a Fae thing, that more of them could feel each other. I'd *felt* him. We'd fought together like a team, completely in tune with each other.

"That's not something we do, Ellie," Nylah said.

She focused her attention on my wounds again, but her concerned expression stayed in place.

"Is it a bad thing?"

She hesitated before shaking her head. "Not at all."

I wanted to know what it meant. I wanted to know why she'd reacted so strangely when I'd asked about it. I didn't have the courage to ask more questions. Not now, when everything around me felt shaky, like my world would fall apart.

Besides, it was out of line.

I was a mere human, here at the mercy of the Fae king. I was an *asset*. Nothing more.

Thinking about him the way I did, the feelings I harbored...

It was wrong.

Rainier was spoken for. He was with Lucia, ready to create a future together for the sake of Jasfin.

Nylah and the King were good friends, too. I couldn't talk to her about this. I knew whose side she would take, and with good reason. It was better to let it all go and forget.

I wanted to forget all of it. The fight today. The connection. The attraction I felt when I was around him.

I just wasn't sure I could forget about something that had been so powerful.

15

I was here for a reason—to become a warrior. Rainier himself had said that I was an asset. I had to get used to the idea of being a warrior and all that it implied. That included fighting, harming, killing if the need arose.

It took me a short while to wrap my mind around it.

"These aren't innocent beings who don't know what hit them," Nylah explained to me. "They know full well what they're getting themselves into. You're not shedding innocent blood. It's kill or be killed. This is exactly what they mean when they say, 'all is fair in love and war.'"

When she put it that way, I understood. They hadn't forced me to be here. I could leave and choose not to kill, but so could the others. I could die just as easily as the rest of them. I wasn't here to stay alive. That might have been the case when I'd arrived. I'd chosen to stay because life here was better than what I'd had back at Steepholde. Now, it wasn't about my survival. It was about the King.

Whenever I looked at him, I felt a strong connection. I was tied to him in a way I didn't understand, and I fiercely needed to protect him.

I didn't understand it; we were nothing to each other. I was a mere human, and he was the Fae king. He had his elite guard to look out for him, too, but I couldn't walk away. I wanted to be there for him, even when the feeling wasn't mutual.

I'd started looking out for him, rather than myself. It made no sense. I was the only one in my life I'd had to look out for all these years.

Everything had changed when they'd brought me here.

When I understood the concept, when I wrapped my mind around what it really meant, it all became clear to me. The guilt of taking lives fell away.

The door to my room opened after I climbed out of the shower, and Bessie came in.

"The meal you sent for, my lady," she said.

"Thank you, Bessie. I'll have it in a moment."

"I don't think there's enough salt. Would you let me add some more?"

"Please, do what you think is right," I said.

Another servant arrived, and I turned to give him my attention. He delivered a new training schedule. Until now, I'd worked only in the mornings, taking part in private sessions with Nylah and Dex. Now, I was going to join the afternoon sessions with the rest of the warriors. It was time to prepare for war.

The idea sent a thrill of excitement through me, paired with a sense of dread.

"Dex asked me to tell you—"

A strange gurgling sound interrupted the messenger's words, and Bessie fell to the floor. She clutched her throat.

"Bessie!" I shouted and fell to my knees at her side. "What's happening? Is she choking?" Panic tightened my chest, and I lowered my ear to her mouth.

I tried to listen to her breathing, but her airways didn't seem obstructed.

"Bessie!" I cried out.

I tried turning her onto her side, but she convulsed, and foamed bubbled out of her mouth. Her eyes became bloodshot, widening, and rolled around wildly in her sockets. She flailed, grabbing for something —anything—that could anchor her. I grabbed her hand and tried to keep her calm, but her eyes filled with fear, and her face turned a strange ashen color.

"Oh, no, back away, my lady," the messenger said, grabbing me around the shoulders and pulling me back. I refused to let go of her, and I was torn between the servant at my back and Bessie. "That's not choking. That's poison."

"What?" I watched as Bessie's body went limp. My throat squeezed shut, and my eyes burned. "How is that possible?" My words came out choked.

I looked at the plate of food she'd been salting, and the spoon she'd used to taste if it was right. I was sick to my stomach. "Why would someone do such a thing?"

The messenger circled the plate of food as if it could jump up and bite him. He took the spoon and carefully sniffed the food.

"Why would someone take out a servant?" I asked again. I was in a daze. "I don't understand..."

"The poison wasn't meant for our Bessie here," the messenger said, his face solemn. "It was meant for you."

His words hit me like punches. Who would try to poison me?

The messenger left the room, taking the plate with him, and I stood in the corner, staring at Bessie's body. She would get up at any moment now, I told myself. This was just some kind of sick joke, a prank the other warriors were playing on me because I was new to the team. This wasn't real.

When Rainier and Nylah came into the room, their faces were grim. Nylah came to me and led me away while the King took care of whatever needed to be done.

"We'll find you a new servant," Nylah said.

I shook my head. "I don't want a new servant."

"Ellie..."

"You can't just replace us, Nylah!" I snapped. "We're not disposable. Humans, I mean, you can't just replace us without a second thought."

"I didn't mean that you are," she said.

I nodded deftly. It had been too close, and Bessie was gone.

"This was another assassination attempt," I said, finally. "Someone is trying to kill me."

Nylah nodded. "We won't let that happen."

"Bessie was just salting my food. If she wasn't so attentive, if she didn't care if I liked it or not, or if I ate in the hall with the others and something like this happened..." I took a deep breath. "I could be dead. Now, someone else is dead because of me—someone with a giant heart and a kind soul." I looked at Nylah. The full weight of what I was saying hit me. "Nylah, what's going on?"

My head spun. Someone wanted me dead. Someone had tried very hard to take me out. It hadn't been the first attempt on my life.

"What if it was Lucia?" I asked.

Nylah pursed her lips. "It wasn't Lucia."

"How do you know? She tried to kill me before."

"You can't talk like that. It's treason."

"Why are you defending her when you know what she tried to do to me that day in training?"

She kept shaking her head, her jaw clenched. "Lucia wouldn't poison you. If she wanted to kill you, she would do it herself."

How reassuring.

"And risk losing Rainier over it? Or doesn't it matter all that much because I'm just a human, anyway? You can all afford to lose me, right? No harm, no foul."

I was angry.

"Stop it, Ellie," Nylah scolded me. "Let's just find out what's going on, okay? I'll suggest to Rainier that he should investigate Lucia."

I didn't believe her. For the first time since I'd arrived, I wasn't sure she had my back on this. I was the human, the outsider. They were still a closed little group.

Fae.

"She's messing with your minds. All of you."

"She can't do that. She's Fae, like the rest of us."

Or Conjurite.

Nylah must have sensed my emotions. She put a hand on my shoulder, her expression gentle.

"We're going to figure it out," she promised. "We're going to look after you, and we're going to make sure they don't get to you. You're important, Ellie. You're important as a member of our warrior family.

You're important to Dex and Ren. And you're important to me. Your friendship is one that I have already come to cherish, and I don't want to lose you."

I still felt sick. Bessie had been *just* a servant, but she'd been sweet and caring. Bessie's life had meaning. I'd been a servant, too. I knew what it was like to work in service, and I knew what it was like to be treated poorly. I'd felt a sort of resonance with her.

And now she'd died in my place.

My throat swelled shut, and my eyes stung with tears. *She* wasn't an example of a warrior who'd known the risks. Hers had been innocent blood spilled, and it wasn't right.

That night, I lay in bed, the curtains wide open. The moonlight fell into the room, a silver stream of light. I couldn't sleep.

I climbed out of bed and tiptoed to the door. When I opened it, Zita stood outside, dressed in leathers, a sword strapped to her hip.

"You're not supposed to be awake," she said.

"I couldn't sleep. I was hoping it would be you out here."

Rainier had ordered warriors to guard my door. It had felt wrong when he'd suggested it—not only was I human, below the other Fae warriors on the food chain, but I had no magic. Now, I wasn't only treated as a warrior; I was being guarded as if I was more important than the rest of them.

"What's on your mind?" Zita asked.

I hesitated. Bessie was on my mind, and so was Lucia. But no one knew about Bessie's death. Rainier and Nylah had asked me to keep it under wraps. They didn't want a mass exodus of servants who fled the palace. I wanted to sound the alarm, but Nylah wanted to find out what was going on before we got everyone on edge.

It didn't sit right with me.

"What do you think about the future queen?" I asked.

Zita frowned. "She's powerful enough to rule at the King's side. It's a good match."

"Do you like her?"

She shrugged. "I don't have to like her. I don't answer to her."

"So, you don't like her?"

Her eyes were dark in the night. "You should be careful what you say."

"Why does everyone tell me that?"

"It's for your own good. Lucia is your queen, or she will be someday soon. You can't turn against her. We're the elite guard. Treason means death, you know."

I nodded. I just didn't understand why everyone was so protective of Lucia.

"You should get some sleep. We're training hard tomorrow. I hear you're joining us."

The training schedule. I'd never looked at it after what had happened to Bessie.

"Goodnight," I said.

Zita was right—I couldn't do much else, and if I was well-rested, at least I could be sharp enough to notice if anything was out of place.

Like poison in my food, for instance—or an attack.

I crawled into bed and closed my eyes, trying to let the tension ease out of my body. I took deep breaths and focused on the air, leaving my lungs flowing through my nose and mouth.

The door slowly opened, and I frowned, sitting up.

"Who is it?" I asked. "Zita?"

"My lady," I heard a soft, familiar voice.

I blinked. Bessie, alive and well, walked into the room. Her cheeks were rosy, and her light, mousy hair was almost silver in the moonlight.

"Bessie?" I asked, incredulous. "But how...?"

My stomach lurched. A sense of doom curled at the pit of my stomach.

"I wanted to make sure you were all right, my lady," she said, the way she had every night before going to bed herself, but this was all wrong.

It was the early hours of the morning, not late at night. Besides, Bessie was dead.

I was seeing things. Ghosts. Her death had terrified me.

The magic was faint at first, but it grew, uncoiling like a snake. When Bessie threw power at me, I sank into my focus right away and blocked the magic.

"No!" I shouted. "Imposter!"

"They won't hear you," the attacker hissed. Even though the assailant wore Bessie's appearance, it wasn't her. I could tell now. I couldn't believe I'd thought she'd come back from the dead a moment earlier. This had to be another spell like what had been done to me. "Your room has been hexed. You're stuck with me, *human*."

Another wave of power came toward me, and I blocked it as best as I could. The wave was strong, but I was used to being attacked by now —I'd trained for this—and my body responded on instinct. I warded off the magical attack and jumped out of bed. I spun around and planted a well-aimed kick to the imposter's gut, sending her flying backward. When she hit the door, her head knocked against it so hard, the image of Bessie blurred, jolted, and then disappeared. In its place sat a short, stocky male with a snarl on his face and eyes the color of oil.

He pulled himself up and attacked again, using magic while he reached for me with clawed hands. I'd never seen hands so ugly, with claws that looked like that of a monster, and teeth that seemed to drip menace.

We fought when he reached me, and it was a combination of well-aimed punches and kicks with waves of magic.

It was tough. An attack by a stranger differed from getting to know the patterns of Dex and Nylah as they trained me. I had to think fast and rely on my strength and my reflexes.

He was on me again and again, fighting me physically, draining my strength with his magic at the same time, so I felt like I was fading, become transparent. I had to act now if I wanted to survive.

"Zita!" I shouted, but she didn't come to my aid.

I fought through the waves of magic that rolled over me, getting closer and closer to the attacker. When I was right in front of him, I hit him as hard as I could, elbowing him in the nose the way I'd done to countless assholes at the tavern who'd groped me.

He staggered, eyes widened in surprise that I'd gotten through the magic.

I hit him once more, and this time, it knocked him out. He fell against my door, unconscious. Blood spilled from his nose, and a bruise formed around his eye, darkening in the silver light of the moon falling into my room—the only light we'd had to fight by.

I shoved him away and opened my door.

"Guards!" I shouted. "Imposter!"

Now that the door was open, and the spell had only been cast on my room, they could hear me, and they came running. Zita was there first. Four guards piled into my room after her.

"What in the seven realms of hell?" she cried out. She looked at me with owlish eyes. "How did he get in?"

We watched as the four males dragged out the unconscious attacker.

My hands trembled, and my body was heavy.

"He was disguised as Bessie," I said and swallowed hard.

"I let her in, thinking it was safe," Zita said.

"She died earlier today. I was told to keep that information to myself, and look was happened."

She frowned at me, but she didn't speak her mind.

It didn't take long before Rainier, Lucia, Dex, and Nylah were all in the hallway in front of my room, talking about what had happened.

Dex asked me questions. Nylah spoke to another servant, unraveling the spells on my room, talking about the spell of disguise that had been used.

I stared at Lucia.

She looked as concerned as the rest of them. Was she?

This couldn't have been her. The attacker had looked like Bessie—it had been the same spell someone had used on me. Lucia was doing something wrong. She used her magic to stay in power. I was sure of it, but this attack had been something different.

Rainier and Lucia discussed getting the word out about Bessie's death to stop another attempt. She'd been allowed into the palace because the other servants hadn't known about her death. They'd thought it was her.

I listened in a daze.

Finally, after making sure I was safe and everything was okay, everyone dispersed. Only Rainier stayed behind.

"We're going to get to the bottom of this," he said curtly.

I nodded.

He turned and left without so much as another word.

Zita stepped into my room.

"Are you okay?" she asked.

"He didn't tell me he's proud of me." I stared down the hallway where Rainier had disappeared.

"Did you expect him to?" she asked.

I looked at her. "I fended for myself when there was no one else to help me."

"You did good, Ellie," Zita said. "But we don't get medals for doing our job."

"You call surviving my *job*?" I cried out. "I was just attacked in my bed! And now that you know about Bessie... It wasn't the first time today that someone tried to kill me."

Zita only nodded.

I had learned to stand up for myself, and I was more confident than ever that I could look after myself.

I'd hoped Rainier would see it, too. But he was detached and business oriented. This needed to be solved, and nothing else.

"You're emotional, and with good reason. You should rest. Everything will look different in the light of day."

"Will the target be gone?" I snapped.

Zita didn't answer.

When I turned back into my room, the disillusion hit me. I was just a warrior, one of many. To Rainier, I wasn't special. In fact, it seemed like I was bringing a lot more trouble to the palace than there'd been before. I'd hoped I was someone special in his eyes, but it was a wake-up call. I was just a human, coming from a small village. Inconsequential. If I disappeared tomorrow, Rainier's life would continue without a hitch.

I had to stop looking for something more when there wasn't anything to be found.

What was I still doing here? Searching for a better life? I might have hated my life at the tavern, but being groped was a far cry from being killed. Was this really that much better? Was there a point in me staying on?

16

"You asked for me, Your Highness?" I stepped into the office where Nylah had taken me to meet the King when he'd offered me the position as a warrior for his guard.

"Ellie, come in," he said with a smile.

I stepped into the office and closed the door. Rainier walked to two large armchairs that faced a fireplace. A fire hadn't been lit, but it was cozy and surrounded by books. How much time did he spend here? I would have been in these chairs all day if I'd had the chance.

Rainier gestured for me to sit in one chair.

I looked at him expectantly. I wasn't sure why I'd been called, but I hoped the King had found out more about the attacks that had happened recently.

"I don't have any answers for you," Rainier said, as if he could read my mind. "I'm sorry."

"That's okay," I said. "I didn't think it was going to be very easy. It seems very delicately planned."

"What makes you say that?" he asked.

"Some of the attacks were arranged by beings inside the palace. Someone knows more than just where I'm going to be and when. They knew what Bessie looked like. They also knew to lock up the warriors when the first attack came from the 'messengers.'"

Rainier nodded and rubbed his chin. He stared into the fireplace as if flames were present to capture his attention.

"I was hoping we could talk a bit. I want to get to know more about you."

I was weary. Why did Rainier want to know more? I knew what he thought of me. He respected me, and he was pleased with my progress as a warrior, but there wasn't anything more. No matter how much I thought we had a connection, we didn't. It was probably like that with everyone he was around. The intense need to protect him, comfort him, be by him...

It had to be every quality a Fae king possessed or was able to radiate. I'd read too far into it when I shouldn't have. I knew better.

Rainier was a Fae king. Royalty. Practically a god.

I was just Ellie, a human that could make a mean drink and defend myself from assholes who thought my breasts were stress balls.

"I want to know if there's something in your past that may lead us down a path I hadn't considered yet," Rainier admitted, and I slouched further into the chair. "I'm stuck on this one, Ellie. I'm going to be frank with you. I don't know what's going on, and it's frustrating as hell. I like to be in control. I like to keep my citizens safe, and there's been too much death and destruction to my liking. We're not even at war yet!"

He was upset. I couldn't feel it the way I had before, but I finally understood it. It came down to him as the ruler to take care of it. Everything was like that—the head was the one that bore the weight of responsibility, and I was the unsolved mystery and, frankly, the weak link. No wonder the King showed up to my training when he had so many more responsibilities. No wonder some Fae wanted me dead. I was the idiot who happened to kill a beast that no one else had and just couldn't die. I was also the moron that thought the King and I had a special connection.

So fucking stupid.

"What do you want to know?" I asked, rubbing my forehead.

Nothing about my past was worth knowing. Hell, my past before this was embarrassing as shit.

"Tell me about yourself," Rainier said. "Just...tell me your story. Don't try to find something significant. I just want to know more."

I held back my groan. I wished I'd had a story worthy of being told, one that I could look back and be proud of, all the accomplishments I'd gained despite adversity. I didn't. I was worthless.

"I don't have a very exciting story to tell. I was abandoned as a child, so I don't know my parents. I was left on the doorstep of an orphanage when I was too young to remember, and there wasn't even a note or anything that could tie me to my parents. I know, it's your typical sob story that no one expects to actually be someone's life outside of a novel."

Rainer leaned forward, his brows furrowing. "You don't remember your parents at all?"

I sighed and glanced at the dark, empty fireplace. "Sometimes, I think I dream about her. My mom. But I don't know—maybe I'm just making it up. Scenarios about my past that I wanted to be true, because I'd know where I'd come from."

My voice faded, but my brain filled it in with the words of my foster parents. *Nowhere, you came from nowhere and are nothing. You will never be worth anything more than the dirt on my shoe in this lifetime.*

I shivered that away and went on. "I lived in the orphanage until I was thirteen." In my mind, I went back to the dilapidated building at the edge of town, with the holes in the roof that wouldn't keep out the rain, broken windows that let in the cold, and ragged blankets that did very little to stave off the cold during winter. We shared our meals with rats and crows, and we barely had a chance to bathe if it didn't rain.

"A rich Fae family adopted me, then. I was so happy to get out of there. I imagined it was something like what I'd read in the stories, where the orphan girl gets the loving home she always dreamed of."

"It didn't work out that way," Rainier said softly, knowing what was next, although he didn't know specifics.

I shrugged. "Reality doesn't work that way, does it? They didn't want a daughter. It was easier to find someone to do their dirty work, to be their slave, than to hire someone to do the work. I didn't like it, but it was a roof over my head that didn't leak for a change, and the leftover food I was allowed to eat after the scraps I'd had to fight for at the orphanage was a step up. So, they beat me, and they were awful to me, saying horrible things about who I was and where I came from. But what was the alternative? The orphanage wouldn't have taken me back even if I'd wanted to go. There were too many of us, and not enough of anything to really pull us through. I'm pretty sure that's why they got rid of me, even if this family might not have checked out. It was somewhere for me to be where I wasn't their problem anymore."

When I glanced at Rainier, his eyes were filled with horror. I looked toward the empty fireplace. It was easier not to look at him while I talked. I knew I'd grown up very differently than he had. His horror only reminded me of that.

"I was there until I was sixteen. When the male of the house tried to force himself onto me, I fought back. I hurt him—pretty badly. I was scared of what they would do to me. Or if they didn't do anything to me...what would happen once he healed? So, I left before anything could go wrong."

For a moment, I thought about that bald asshole, with his thick fingers and his onion-laced breath. His voice had been harsh in my ear when he'd gotten too close. It hadn't taken much to hit him in the face with a candle holder. It had been a silver one, too, with a hexagonal base that had broken his nose and chipped two teeth. The damage hadn't been enough to keep him down, just enough for me to get away. To run.

I could still taste the fear at the back of my throat when I thought about it. I could still smell the onion on his breath.

I wrapped my arms around myself. "I found work as a barmaid. The owner wasn't great, but he wasn't mean, which was a step up. He couldn't pay me, but I was allowed to stay in a small room above the bar. He fed me most days, and I could keep the tips I made. It wasn't bad. It was warmer than being on the street, and I could buy extra food sometimes when I made enough in tips. No one could dictate how I lived my life anymore. That was a big deal to me. It was a shitty life, but it was mine."

I glanced at Rainier again, and his eyes were filled with pity this time. I hated pity.

"Don't look at me like that," I said. "Not everyone is born into a shiny palace."

His face steeled at that. "I know your life has been hard, but we all have tough times we need to go through."

"Sorry," I said. "You're right. Just because you were born in a palace does not mean your life has been easy."

Thinking back to my past hurt. I didn't like revisiting the hell I'd been through. Now that I was here, living in a decent room with a future, I didn't want to look back anymore. I didn't know how any of this would help Rainier, but if he could find answers...

It was the only reason I was telling him.

"You learned to fight," Rainier said. "When did this happen?"

"At the bar," I said. "I had to fend off males who were too drunk to remember their manners and decided I was a nice piece to have on the side. They would get into bar fights, too, and I usually broke them up. It saved whatever cups and plates were going to break so that I didn't have to pay for them from the tips I made." I shrugged. "We do what we need to do to survive, Your Highness."

"Please, you don't have to be so formal with me," Rainier said. "You can call me Ren when we're in private."

"What?"

"My friends call me Ren. In public, when respect is deserved, you can refer to me as Your Highness, King Rainier, or whatever other title I'm called. But when it's just us..."

He wanted me to call him Ren. Only his close friends called him Ren. I'd thought he wanted to keep me at arm's length, but it turned out there was more than just me being a warrior in his guard.

"I'm sorry you've been through such a tough time," he said.

"I'm sorry my past won't offer you any answers to the questions you're asking," I countered.

Ren sighed. "It's okay. I didn't think much could come of it. It was a shot in the dark, but I'm glad you told me. It helps me understand you better."

I wasn't sure what to make of what he said, but the atmosphere between us had shifted and changed. It was warm now, comfortable. It wasn't an interview with the King anymore. Rather, it was two friends talking.

"Thank you for coming to see me," Ren finally said and stood.

The meeting was over. I was being dismissed.

"I'll figure out what's going on, still. I just need to understand where to start digging."

"We'll do what we can to help," I said.

"I know. I have a group of very loyal Fae in my life. If we put our strengths together, I'm sure we'll find the answers to who you are and why you're so important that someone is out to get you."

I nodded and left his office. He was right—I wasn't a threat.

And yet, someone wanted me dead.

17

Nylah and I sat around the large table in a conference room when Ren and Lucia entered. Ren looked solemn. He wore casual attire—comfortable pants and a tunic—where Lucia behind him looked like she was ready to host a royal dinner.

"Thank you for coming," he said to us warmly. He pulled out a chair for Lucia, who sat down, eyeing the two of us.

Ren sat down next to her, but he turned slightly away from her. He rang for a servant and ordered tea, pitchers of water, and plates with finger food for us to snack on.

It looked like it was going to be a long afternoon.

"We need to discuss the probability that these attacks are directly from Palgia," he continued after the servants brought in his orders and we were alone again. He looked at Lucia. "We keep looking at other sources, but what if this is already the war we've been waiting for?"

"Is the attack from Palgia that imminent?" Nylah asked.

Ren opened his mouth to answer, but Lucia spoke before he could say anything.

"Why is she here?" she asked, looking at me.

Ren seemed irritated. "Ellie is an integral part of the war."

"Because she's the one that's being attacked? It might be easier to offer her up and get it over with, have all this trouble end. Don't you think?" She smiled as if it was a joke, but it didn't reach her eyes.

I shifted uncomfortably in my seat. Next to me, Nylah bristled with anger, too.

"That's not happening," Ren said bluntly. She pouted, but he continued talking without paying attention to her. "Ellie is a crucial part in liaising with the humans."

I nodded. Nylah had mentioned this to me a short while ago, and I wanted to do what I could to help. A lot of the free humans lived in the Uprain Mountains between Jasfin and Palgia.

Lucia snorted. "And since when can the humans help us?"

"The humans in the mountains interact with Fae from both kingdoms," Nylah explained, talking to Lucia simply as if she were a child. "If Ellie can gain knowledge from them, it might help."

"Humans don't trust the Fae," Ren added.

Lucia rolled her eyes and huffed. "I can't see why. We've been nothing but good to them, taking care of them, giving them jobs. They'd be nothing without us."

"And a lot of humans are slaves," I pointed out. "There are few free humans in the Fae villages. I wouldn't trust the Fae, either, if I didn't know what it could be like here at the palace. It's only now that Ren is on the throne—"

"*What* did you just call him?" Lucia sneered with narrowed eyes. "Ren? That's *Your Highness* to you. Who do you think you are, you little cretin?"

I wanted to respond, but it was Ren who got there first.

"That's enough!" he barked. "I told her she could call me Ren. She's on our side, Lucia. Not everyone in the palace is a threat."

"You can understand why I've been wary, my love," Lucia said in a small voice. "With so many attacks, who can feel safe anymore? And it all started with her arrival." She pointed a slim finger in my direction.

"We're going to figure out what's going on, but she's going to help us, no matter which way you want to look at it. Ellie isn't leaving."

Lucia huffed and sat back in her chair, sulking like a child. She was manipulative, and I had the idea she was used to getting what she wanted. Ren wasn't indulging her whims, and it looked like she wasn't happy about that.

"Where were we?" Ren asked, looking back at us.

"It's no secret King Falx of Palgia has wanted the resources in Jasfin," Nylah said. "I'm sure he'll stop at nothing, and now that he's getting more and more powerful, I think it's right to ready ourselves for an attack."

"What do we have that they don't?" I asked.

Lucia responded, "Everything. Don't you know that?"

"There are mines with magical gemstones in them," Ren said, ignoring her.

"And the rich lands where they could farm, the luscious forests and running water," Nylah added. "Jasfin is a rich land, looked after by its citizens for centuries, where Palgia just let their country go to ruin. The Conjurite magic has been a big part of their demise. The dark magic brings death and destruction—even if it can take a long time."

"Right," I said.

I remembered Nylah explaining it to me that way. When I'd arrived here, it had all seemed so surreal, like part of a fairy tale. The more I became a part of this world, the more I realized it was all very real. And it had become real to me. This was my home now, after all.

"We have to be careful when we counter an attack," Ren said. "With the Uprain Mountains in the middle, we'll have to be careful about losing human lives. Palgia won't hesitate to crush anything and anyone in its path, humans and fairies alike."

"Why don't we use the humans as shields?" Lucia asked.

My chest constricted. "What?" I demanded, breathless.

"If we sacrifice them first, it will wear out the Palgians. By the time we get there, we can win the war."

"So..." I was struggling to wrap my mind around what she was saying. Blood rushed in my ears, and anger and indignation burned hot on my skin. "You're suggesting we sacrifice the humans for the sake of an easy win?"

Lucia shrugged. "Once I'm queen, humans won't keep the same liberties they now enjoy."

"What are you talking about?" I shot back. "Some humans still exist as slaves in Jasfin. They don't have any liberties."

Lucia offered a sly look. "Enslaving the humans is the right thing to do, and it's what the Fae have done for very long time. Palgia isn't giving up that practice anytime soon. Humans are lesser beings. Why mess with the way things are? It's worked for centuries."

"Has it?" I challenged. "It's easy to say when you're not a slave." My whole life, the Fae had oppressed me because I was a *lesser being*. I'd had to fight for a roof over my head, food in my belly, my basic right to *survive* because someone had decided we weren't good enough, while Lucia lived a carefree, comfortable life surrounded by luxury.

What would she do if she had to fend for herself, even just for a day? She would lie down and die.

Lucia shook her head, irritated. "Will you blame me for my birthright?" She put her hand on Ren's arm, her eyes finding his. "It's high time Jasfin makes all humans slaves again, instead of working toward their freedom."

I couldn't believe it. My chest was tight, and I struggled to breathe. My ears rang, and anger flashed red before my eyes.

"You're a heartless bitch!" I cried out.

Lucia jumped up. "Careful how you talk to me, little rat," she sneered. "I flattened you before. I can do it again."

"I'd like to see you try," I challenged. My ire was in control now. If she attacked me, I didn't know what I would do.

Before I could act, Lucia slammed a powerful wave of magic into me. It hit me so hard, I flew back, my chair toppling over, and I hit the far wall of the room. Lucia was in front of me in the blink of an eye. She held her hands up, curled as if she were strangling me, but she wasn't touching me. Her fingers were curled around air.

It didn't feel that way. She was squeezing the life out of me. Her magic was so powerful, it forced its way into my body and caused every vessel to constrict. Lucia wasn't only strangling my neck, she was strangling every inch of me with her magic.

Nylah and Ren jumped into action. Ren threw a powerful spell between me and Lucia, and it shoved her back. I gasped for air as everything opened again, and I could breathe.

"That's enough!" Ren shouted, and he bound Lucia's hands with magic.

She screamed, and I felt her fighting the bonds, trying to break it with her own magic. But she didn't have enough of it—Ren was far more powerful than she was.

When he did, it was like a veil lifted. I could feel it drawing back, and Ren and Nylah both took a deep breath. They blinked as if they'd just woken up. They stared at each other.

Ren's eyes were wide, but anger replaced the surprise, and his lips twisted in a snarl. "What have you done?"

He grabbed Lucia by the arm and dragged her out of the room.

"Are you okay?" Nylah asked, kneeling next to me. She looked at me, concerned, eyes flitting over my face and body to see if there was any damage she wasn't aware of.

"I'm okay," I gasped and coughed. "I just need a moment."

Nylah nodded and sat back.

"Courageous to call her a bitch," she said.

"Someone had to do it."

Nylah chuckled. "Yeah...I wish it had been me."

"Really, you don't." I rubbed my hand across my throat. The ghost of her hands were still wrapped around me there, even though she hadn't touched me at all.

From the next room, we heard Ren and Lucia shouting at each other. The words weren't clear, but we could hear their tones. Lucia wasn't happy, but Ren was furious.

"I don't think I've ever heard him this angry," Nylah said in a low voice.

"I'm surprised he's not taking me out for what I said."

"She did something," Nylah said. She rubbed the back of her neck. "When he bound her hands, tying up her magic... She had a spell on all of us."

"You didn't feel it before?"

Nylah shook her head and closed her eyes. She frowned, concern filling her face. She sucked her bottom lip into her mouth and worried about it as she thought.

"I should have known something was wrong. I feel like I've been asleep, and I just woke up. We've never had a reason to tie her magic like that before, and I'm willing to wager she counted on that. You tried to tell me, didn't you? That's what you meant." Nylah let out a frustrated sigh. "This isn't our magic."

"Conjurite," I said.

She shot me a sharp look. "We don't accuse Fae of that, not unless we know for sure. It's a terrible thing."

Lucia was a terrible thing. Couldn't they see?

"I think Ren is on your side with this one. It's about time." She smirked at me. Nylah disliked Lucia every bit as much as I did. She'd respected Ren's choices because they were close, but she didn't like Lucia at all.

The shouting escalated, followed by a deafening crash.

Nylah and I jumped up at the same time and raced for the door.

When she yanked it open, Ren stood before a large hole in the wall. His jaw was clenched, and his eyes were the color of ice.

"She's gone," he said in a bitter tone.

"Oh, no," Nylah breathed.

Ren looked at me, and cold washed through my body. His anger was very different from what I'd seen before. He was pale, his skin tight and paper thin so I could see the shape of his skull. His magic danced in the air around us, alive, breathing on its own. His emotions were everywhere, scattered across the room. I *felt* it.

Without another word, he turned and left the room, leaving me and Nylah behind, staring at the damage Lucia had left in her wake.

18

I walked into the palace library and looked up at the towering bookcases. The library ceiling had to be three stories high, and the bookcases ran all around the room, stretching all the way to the top. The curtains covered dark windows, but a storm raged outside, rain pattering against the windowpanes.

The library lights were on, grand chandeliers hanging far above me. The plush carpet was a deep red underneath my feet.

Ladders and balconies allowed anyone to reach the top books. In the center of the room, comfortable couches created an intimate circle, with side tables and a coffee table. It looked cozy, and I wanted to curl up there with a book to forget about everything that was happening in my life.

I walked along one shelf, letting my fingers play over the spines. Most of the covers were cloth. It looked like a lot of first editions and rare books, impossible to find anywhere else.

I'd been to Nylah's library a few times, and I had a small collection of books in the bookcase in my room, but this was spectacular. I'd never seen so many books in one room in my life.

I walked along one shelf and picked a book to read that I'd never heard of before. I ran my fingers over the cover, tracing the dim letters that had been worn away with years of use.

The couches were as comfortable as they looked, and I sank into the cushions with a sigh. I opened the book and started reading. I let the story transport me to another world.

"Ellie?"

Ren's voice was right next to me, and I jumped. I twisted in the seat. Ren stood a short distance away, looking apologetic.

"Sorry," he said. "I didn't mean to scare you."

"I was...lost," I said. "In the book."

I closed it and put it down on the coffee table. Ren came closer, but he didn't sit down. Emotions warred in his eyes, and he pressed his lips in a thin line.

"You can sit down," I offered.

He hesitated before he took a seat next to me. He leaned his elbows on his knees, steepling his fingers.

"I want to talk to you about what Lucia did this afternoon, and about what she said."

The fallout had been awkward, but Lucia was evil. It wasn't Ren's fault.

I nodded slowly.

"She had us all under a spell." He took a breath and let it out slowly. It looked like it was hard for him to admit it. "Nylah says you warned her."

"I didn't know for sure. It was just a feeling."

"A feeling."

I nodded.

"I should have seen it," he said, looking at his hands. "I didn't know, but I should have."

"The nature of her spell made it impossible to know," I assured him, not wanting him to beat himself up about it. "You didn't *allow* it."

"I know," Ren said. "But she's the future queen. *Was.* Whatever she does reflects on me, and I want you to know that her thoughts about the humans..." He swallowed hard. "I didn't know that she planned to harm them. I didn't realize we weren't on the same page. Not only with leadership, but in morals and values, too." He sighed and glanced up at me. "She has a dark heart. I didn't see it. I don't know how I could have missed it. After all this time...it's not like love blinded me."

"People—and Fae—don't always show their true colors right away," I said.

He smiled at me. "It's good of you to say, but I feel like this one is on me. I should be better. As king, I should know better than that. I was so focused on everything coming at us from the outside, I didn't think to look right next to me."

"You know now, and that's what matters," I said. "This way, you know what you're getting yourself into when you marry her."

"I will not marry her. It's over between us."

"What?" I asked. "What about the political alliance?" It had to be important if he had been willing to spend the rest of his life with someone for the sake of it.

Ren shook his head. "I don't care about that. She's not right to rule as queen. It's our job to protect our citizens, not *use* them to our bene-fit. This whole slavery idea every king has indulged since the beginning of time...that has to stop, too. Humans deserve to be free. I am sitting down with my advisors this week to figure out a plan."

I stared at him. Did he care that much about humans? I saw a different side of Ren—a much softer, caring side. I liked what I saw. He wasn't nearly as hard and cold as he made himself out to be.

"Can't you just make it a law that humans can't be enslaved?" I asked.

"Of course, and I plan on doing that. However, where will the slaves go? How will they earn a living? It's actually quite complicated, and that's why I want you involved. I want you to help secure their freedom."

"I will do anything you ask of me." And that was true. I trusted Ren; he had a just and fair heart.

"I want to apologize to you for everything Lucia put you through. I should have seen her first attempt on your life as the red flag that it was." He looked like he felt foolish. "Lucia can be very convincing. She plays the innocent victim all too well. I should have seen through her lies."

"It's all right," I said. "You did the right thing. Again, it's rather that, than only finding out after you're married and there's nothing you can do."

"You're very positive about everything, when your life was in danger each time."

I shrugged. "Day in the life of Ellie."

Ren chuckled and shook his head. He reached for my red locks and brushed my hair over my shoulder.

"I'm glad to have you here, Ellie," he said. "You're a breath of fresh air I didn't realize I needed. I don't know who enchanted you to look like Zander to frame you for my father's death, but I'm happy that it brought you here."

My cheeks flushed. He was being so open with me. I wasn't used to his warmth. Ren was so cold so often.

"I'm glad to be here," I said. My voice was breathy, and my heart thrummed in my throat.

Ren's eyes slid down my face and to my lips. Time stopped around us, and it enveloped us in a bubble, where the rest of the world didn't exist.

This time, Ren didn't clear his throat and turn away. He didn't shut down from me. Instead, he leaned in, closing the distance between us.

His lips brushed against mine, and my breath caught in my throat. He kissed me, and electricity pulsed through my body. Ren cupped my cheek, and power quivered between us—more powerful than anything I'd felt before. Heat stretched thin between us, and yet it was cool to the touch. It wrapped itself around us, and my body hummed at the same frequency Ren's did.

He broke the kiss. I stared at him, dazed and out of breath. His eyes filled with warmth and something...dark, but the delicious kind.

I shivered. My whole body felt awake, every nerve bursting with life.

"Good night, Ellie," he said and stood. He rubbed his hands together and cleared his throat.

"Good night," I said in a thin voice.

Where was he going? I wanted to finish what we'd started. I wanted to feel his hands on my skin. I wanted to feel his kisses on every inch of my body. I wanted...more.

When he left the library, I fell back against the pillows, covered my face with my hands, and melted into a puddle.

19

I was up before dawn, had breakfast in the mess hall, and headed out to the training arena, where Dex and Nylah waited for me. We started working through our drills, with Nylah and Dex both throwing magic at me.

Halfway through, Nylah grinned at Dex before they both looked at me.

"What?" I asked.

"You're doing great," she said. "I think our job here is done."

"What do you mean?" I asked.

"You'll train with the guard now. Any other private sessions you'll have will be with Ren."

"I don't get to see you both every morning anymore?" I asked.

Dex's mouth only twitched. I didn't think he'd ever smiled in his life.

"You can always come see me at the cathedral. You're not leaving, just progressing."

I nodded. I knew what Nylah was saying, but the thought of not having morning sessions with her and Dex felt like a loss. She was right, though. I could visit them whenever I wanted to. With everything going on, it wasn't like we wouldn't work together.

After our training sessions, I walked to my room to shower and get dressed to go to lunch.

A servant stopped me. "The King requests your presence," he said.

"Right now?"

He nodded. My stomach fluttered, and I turned, walking to Ren's office. I was nervous to see him. I wished he would have let me see him after getting clean. I looked terrible now—sweaty and dirty after training hard. Ren had seen me like this dozens of times, and I hadn't cared, but after last night, it was different. I *wanted* to look nice for him.

I took a deep breath and knocked on the door. When Ren called for me to enter, I opened the door and closed it behind me. I smiled at Ren, who sat behind his desk. He finished whatever he was writing and stood. He didn't come around the desk to greet me. His eyes were cold and hard. All the warmth from the previous night in the library was gone.

"Thank you for coming to see me," he said. "I want to talk to you about last night." I swallowed, and my stomach erupted in butterflies. "I'm sorry I kissed you."

The apology was like a punch to my gut.

"What?"

"My behavior was wrong. I'm sorry about that. It won't happen again."

My heart sank. Ren looked so solemn. Did he really think it was a mistake?

"It's...okay," I replied.

Couldn't I think of anything else to say? I wanted to tell him I'd liked it. That I'd wanted it. I just had to say it.

But what future did we have? He was the Fae King of Jasfin, and no matter how much I liked him and how it had affected me when he'd kissed me, it would never change the fact that I was a human.

"We won't talk about it again," I added, squaring my shoulders.

"Thank you," Ren said. "I appreciate you're not making a fuss."

"You're used to women making a fuss," I said.

He nodded. "Sad that it's so, but I've learned my lesson."

"Where is she?" I asked. "Do you know?"

The last we'd seen of her was when she'd blasted a magical hole in the palace's wall and disappeared.

Ren shook his head and looked at a stack of papers in front of him. "She's back home. Her father took her back in. He contacted me this morning to talk."

"Is he upset?" I asked. What happened when an alliance was broken? War? I didn't know if Jasfin could handle that on top of what was happening with Palgia.

"No, he keeps apologizing for her attitude. He wants me to take her back, and he tried to convince me that she just had a slip-up. She gets very emotional sometimes."

I frowned. "You're not taking her back, are you?"

Ren looked at me, raising his eyebrows. Maybe I should have asked it differently, with less disdain at the idea. He was the King of Jasfin— he could do whatever he wanted.

"No. I told her I won't take her back. Apologizing for an outburst is one thing, but we don't see eye to eye, and that's not something she can fix with a few well-aimed words."

I nodded, feeling relieved. Ren regretted kissing me, and that stung. At least he wasn't going to marry Queen Evil. He'd seen Lucia for who she really was, and he'd acted on it. In my eyes, it made him a good king, and a good male.

"Is that all?" I asked when the silence between us stretched so thin I couldn't bear it. I didn't regret last night at all. I'd dreamed about those lips for a while now. It had been more magical than anything I'd envisioned.

Ren nodded. "Thank you for coming to see me," he said the way he had when I'd walked in.

I turned and left the office. The knowledge that the kiss had meant nothing to him hurt. I had to get over this silly little crush I was developing. Because that was exactly what it was—a crush. And nothing would come of it. It wasn't possible, not with who we were and where we came from. Our worlds were too different, and even though Ren had given me a place of honor in the palace and in the guard, it didn't put me on any kind of pedestal. I had to accept that and move on.

THE WATER WAS HOT WHEN I STEPPED INTO THE SHOWER, AND I closed my eyes. I let the water carry away the sweat and the dirt and hoped that it would take my disappointment along with it.

When I climbed out of the shower, I missed Bessie. A pang shot through my chest when I opened my wardrobe. I felt alone. I dressed in a fresh pair of training clothes so that I could train with the guard after lunch. I had a friend in Zita already, so the training was something to look forward to.

And yet, it felt bland. I wasn't as excited as I should have been.

Finally, I walked to the mess hall to eat, my stomach already rumbling.

This was what I was going to focus on—the elite guard and training hard. Preparing to do my job as the King's protector.

I wouldn't think about Ren and Lucia, that he was single now, that he'd kissed me.

In this war, I could still win.

But I would lose the battle against the barriers that kept me and Ren apart.

20

The next morning, I walked into the arena to train, and Ren stood there waiting for me. He wore training clothes. His leathers were casual and embroidered with gold thread—without the gems and jewels that he wore on his royal robes when he had to meet with advisors and pass laws. He looked...normal.

"Morning," I said.

"Good morning. Are you ready to train?"

I nodded, but I didn't feel ready at all.

"Let's warm up," he said.

He put me through a bunch of drills, but where Dex had stood on the sidelines, barking orders, Ren warmed up with me.

"You're training, too," I said after we'd done half an hour of intense cardio to warm up. We stood at the side of the arena, drinking water, breathing hard.

"I don't let my warriors do anything I won't do myself. Some kings believe their armies are there to fight *for* them. They watch from a safe distance. I believe that if I'm asking my warriors to sacrifice their lives for something, I better be willing to do it, too. If I won't do something, how can I expect them to do it?"

I didn't know what to say. The more I got to know Ren, the more I liked him. He was a decent male.

Noble.

Off limits.

Damn it, Ellie, he is off limits!

"Come, let's get started," he said, putting his bottle down. He walked to the center of the arena.

"We're doing hand-to-hand today," he said.

He took a step forward so that our bodies were almost pushed against each other, and his closeness made me feel dizzy. We'd both trained hard and were already sweating, but the scent of his sweat, mixed with the spices of his cologne, was intoxicating.

I sank into a battle stance automatically. I'd done this often enough that even when I wasn't thinking clearly, my body knew what to do. Thank the Goddess, or I was going to look like an idiot.

"Are you ready?" Ren asked.

I nodded. He hit me so fast, I didn't see him move until after the impact. I let out a sharp breath at the pain that blossomed on my arm.

"You're not ready," he said. "You need to focus."

He was right. I wasn't ready. I couldn't afford what I felt for Ren to affect my fighting skills. Shit like that could get me killed.

"Ready?" he repeated.

This time, when he hit me, I blocked the blow and countered, getting a hit on his ribs.

I winced. I'd just hit the King, but Ren laughed.

"That's better." He stepped closer again.

This time, I tried to ignore the heat between us when he was so close to me. I tried to forget about the scent in my nostrils that turned me on, making my body flush with heat. I focused on his movements—fluid and battle-hardened. I tried to predict where he was going, so I could counter him.

Ren's face changed when we fought. Delight filled his eyes, and he loved to be active, loved to move.

And he was damn good at it, too.

His eyes were drowning deep when they locked on mine, and I had to push myself to focus on what he was doing. He threw light spells at me, and I blocked his magic easily. He was taking it easy on me. He was far more powerful than the meager blows he sent my way, but I wouldn't have been able to fight him if he'd used his full strength on me.

When he tried to kick me, I backed out but tripped over my own feet. I stumbled, but Ren was right there, an arm around my waist, stopping me from falling.

I was breathing hard, and his face was close to mine. The connection opened between us as if the block had never been there.

I knew what he was feeling. I knew what he was thinking.

He set me on my feet and attacked again, but this time, I knew where he was going to be. I blocked it and countered, but Ren knew what I was thinking, too. We moved around each other, fighting, but it had become a dance. We were in sync, perfectly connected, and neither of us could land a single blow.

Finally, Ren stopped. He put his hands on his hips, breathing hard.

"That was incredible," he said. "Did you feel that?"

He stepped closer to me. I nodded.

Ren studied my face, his eyes on my lips. I wanted him to kiss me. I wanted him to hold me—to touch me. I wanted him to do anything his imagination could come up with.

Things I had no business wanting from him.

Ren leaned a little closer and lifted his hand. It hovered over my skin, and I ached for his touch. He was about to speak when the door to the warrior's quarters banged open and broke the spell.

Ren stepped back and turned.

"What is it?" he asked.

A male in dark robes and golden chains around his neck came to us. His hair was neatly combed to the side, and his dark robes were finely embroidered with silver thread.

"I'm sorry to bother you, Rainier," he said.

"It's fine," Ren said and glanced at me. "Ellie, this is Leander, one of my advisors. Leander, this is Ellie."

"It's nice to meet you, Leander," I said. I faced Ren. "I'll leave you now, so you can speak to your advisor in private."

"No, it's all right," Leander said. "It's best if you know, being a warrior that will fight for King Rainier's protection." He paused, then faced Ren. "There is a hunter in Jasfin coming for you."

"How do you know?" Ren asked, frowning.

"We felt Conjurite energy in the forest when we were out this morning," the advisor said.

Ren's frown deepened. "A hunter from Palgia."

The advisor nodded. "That's what we believe. We have taken extra measures for your safety but believe it's necessary for you to know."

"It was right to tell me," Ren said. "But a part of me wants to drop the security so that asshole can come in and we can handle it and get it done with."

"That might not be the best course of action," Leander said carefully.

"I know, I know." Ren put his hands on his hips. I couldn't feel him at all now. He'd blocked himself off completely, but he looked troubled...and angry.

"I'm tired of this, and it hasn't even started," he said. "We'll get this taken care of. Let me know if there are any changes. Anything at all."

The advisor bowed and left the training arena.

Ren looked at me, his eyes troubled. We were alone again, but the spell had been broken, and the news of a hunter from Palgia coming here to kill him had spoiled the mood.

I wanted to ask him about the hunter. I wanted to know what he was thinking, but he'd shut me out.

"That's it for training today," Ren said. His mind was already on work, and his voice was empty. "You can go and clean up for lunch. Well done, your skills are coming along nicely."

He walked away. It gutted me. He was so formal now, when we'd been so close. And, the way we'd fought together...

Or rather, we hadn't fought at all, because we'd been completely connected and on the same page. It was hard to have him wide open and present one moment and withdrawn and shut down the next.

I didn't know what to make of it.

I left the training grounds to shower and eat so that I could make it in time for my second training session.

I preferred being trained privately, but war wouldn't be private. I had to get to know my fellow warriors.

It would be better if I focused on that than whatever was happening between me and Ren.

21

I sat in bed, reading one of Nylah's large history books she'd offered to me. In her library, I'd found a lot of books about the history of the country. I'd read all about Jasfin and Palgia. I'd followed Ren's bloodline back to kings and queens that had lived eons before I did. I'd read about the Fae, their power, the Goddess Terra, and everything that was known about the deity.

But there was very little about the Uprain Mountains where the humans lived. The more I searched, the more I came up empty-handed, and that made me more and more curious.

This book was about them—about the civil wars a long time ago, and how the Fae had enslaved humans after they'd lost the war. Without magic, the humans hadn't known which way to turn, and being slaves had been better than leaving their home altogether.

Did they still feel the same? Would they have traded their freedom if they knew what it had meant for the rest of us that had come so long after? Ren wanted me to go to the humans in the Uprain Mountains, to liaise with them and find out what they knew about Palgia. I wanted to know what they felt for the Fae. I was human, but I sided with the Fae. Well, I sided with the Fae now that I knew slavery would soon be abolished. Would the humans hate me? Would they mistrust me?

A knock on the door snapped me back to the present.

"Come in," I called. A servant usually knocked and opened right away.

When the door opened, it was Ren. He looked confused.

"Oh," I said and climbed out of bed. I wrapped a robe around my shoulders and gestured for Ren to join me in my small living room. I sat down in my favorite armchair, and he took a seat opposite me.

"I'm sorry to bother you this late. I didn't want to wait until morning," he said when he sat down.

He didn't look comfortable. He didn't look like he was planning on staying long.

"What's wrong?" I asked, trying to ignore what I felt now that I knew he didn't want me—even though he'd kissed me.

"I'm worried about the Palgian hunter that's roaming the forest. He's waiting for his time to strike."

"Your advisor said he's a Conjurite," I said.

Ren nodded. "That's what I'm worried about. Do you know what a Conjurite is?"

"Nylah taught me a few things when I went to her in the beginning, and I've been reading up about the history of dark magic."

"Good. That's very good. Understanding who we are will help you know what this is all about. The Conjurite magic is powerful. If my advisors could feel it without the hunter being too close...I'm worried about what that means when it comes down to an attack."

"We've all been prepared for it," I said. "We've been training specifically."

Earlier, when I'd trained with the other warriors, Dex had asked Nylah to attack us with more magic so that we could work on blocking and countering as much of it as we could. It had been hard, but it hadn't been impossible.

Nylah's magic wasn't dark magic, so I didn't know what it would really feel like. She'd mentioned it wasn't power she could—or wanted to—duplicate. Even for the sake of training.

Despite not knowing what to expect, I was sure we could handle it.

But Ren shook his head. "It's not enough. I don't want you going up against this assassin when he comes to the palace."

I frowned. "What? Why not?"

"Because he's dangerous. I'm going to send you away for a while, somewhere you'll be safe."

I gasped. "You're getting rid of me?"

"No, that's now how I meant it—"

"You want me gone."

"To keep you safe," Ren said

"What's the point of all of this, then?" I gestured toward the windows that overlooked the arena. "What have I been training for, if you're just going to send me away at the first sign of trouble?"

Ren shook his head and stood, walking to the windows to look out into the dark of the night.

"This isn't the *first* sign of trouble, Ellie. There's been a hell of a lot more than I'm comfortable with, and they've all been aimed at you. This is the first attack—or potential attack—that doesn't have your name on it, and I would like to keep it that way."

"I'm a warrior, here to fight for *you*. To protect you. Isn't that how you wanted it?"

He turned to look at me over his shoulder. "I don't see the point in sending you into the fray, if it's only going to mean it's your end."

I rolled my eyes. I was getting irritated with him. He was being unreasonable, which was very unlike the King I knew.

"I know what it means, Ren. I know it's a sacrifice, but that's what this is all about. "

"You can't go in there. You're more fragile than the Fae."

"Right," I said tightly. "Because I'm not good enough."

"That's not what I said," he snapped.

"Oh, no? When did you decide I was too *frail* to fight in your elite guard? Was it before or after you kept me on?"

"Ellie, this isn't—"

"I stayed here because I believed you when you said I was an asset and that I can handle myself. Now, it turns out I'm only here to make nice with the humans, but you don't trust me to—"

"I can't bear to see you get hurt!" Ren shouted, cutting me off. "Anything can happen, and I can't do that. I...won't put you in danger."

He looked at me, and his expression was raw. His voice cracked when he talked.

He shook his head and walked to the door.

"Ren," I said before he reached it, and he stopped and turned to me. "I won't get hurt out there. You don't have to do this. I want to be a part of it. I want to be useful. This is the first time in my life I've had purpose, the first time I feel like there's something bigger to fight for than getting food in my mouth at night and surviving through the winter."

Ren didn't answer me.

"I trained with Dex and Nylah. You're training me, too. I'm working with the other warriors—if that doesn't prepare me for what's coming, then no one will ever be ready. Dex even said that I'd progressed faster than any of his warriors, and that he's proud to have me on the team."

"He's not wrong. You fight hard, and you give your all," Ren relented.

I sagged a little, relieved that he agreed I was doing well.

"But I won't forgive myself if something happens to you. I want you safe, Ellie."

He turned and left my room, and I stared at the door he'd disappeared through, stunned. My shock turned into anger, and I stood, pacing the room. How could he do this to me? How could he keep me here, making me think I was training to fight for a bigger cause when he didn't want me to get involved?

And how could he tell me how much he cared when he kept pushing me away?

I needed to talk to someone about it. I just didn't know who. I couldn't talk to Nylah—she and Ren were like brother and sister.

And I couldn't talk to Dex, either. What advice would he give me?

I had no one I could talk to about my frustrations. Ren wouldn't let me fight, even though that's why I was at the palace in the first place. Also, I had feelings for him, which seemed to be accepted sometimes and rejected at others.

Instead of talking to anyone, I climbed back into bed and switched off the light. I would read about the humans in the mountains another time. Right now, I wanted to fall asleep. Hopefully, the confusion would be less in the morning, and Ren would have changed his mind.

I wouldn't let him send me away. I belonged here. This had become my home, and I wanted to do what I could to protect it. Nylah was a dear friend, and Dex, albeit perpetually grumpy, had become endearing. I was close to Ren, too—more so now that Lucia was gone. Although he was harder to understand than the rest of them.

After I'd just arrived, I would have fought tooth and nail to prove that I deserved to be here, that it hadn't been a mistake. That had changed to me wanting to fight tooth and nail to save what had become mine.

Ren couldn't send me away. Where would I go? I didn't belong anywhere else. I'd never really belonged anywhere. And now that I finally did, I wouldn't sit down and watch the carnage from the sidelines. I wanted to get into the fray and do what they had trained me to do.

22

Ren and I were in the training arena. It had been a few days since we'd learned of the hunter's presence, and nothing had happened. Ren had been on edge, and the guards had been wide awake, looking for something—anything—that might be out of place.

As the days passed and nothing happened, the Fae at the palace relaxed. Ren started focusing on other business again, and the guards weren't as vigilant as before.

The advisors had gone out again and again, but they'd found no Conjurite.

"Maybe the Conjurite hunter isn't a hunter at all, but just a Conjurite, passing through," I'd suggested to Nylah last night, when I'd visited her in the cathedral.

"Conjurites don't 'pass through' places like Jasfin, where they are enemies," Nylah had said, but she hadn't had a better reason for the hunter to have just disappeared.

Whatever it was, I was glad Ren hadn't me sent away. It seemed like he had decided not to do that, after all. It meant something to me.

Ren and I were going through hand-to-hand drills, working on blocking and countering, over and over. I enjoyed working with him.

He was focused and just as dedicated to working hard as the rest of his warriors. When he asked me to push hard, he pushed harder. When we fought and he expected me to do things that were beyond what I'd thought I could do, he did them first.

We hadn't connected again like we had during that first training session. I'd stopped fretting about what we could be, and what we weren't, and everything in between. I had to accept that nothing would ever change between us, and that was how things were going to be. Ren saw me as a friend, someone he could trust, but he would never see me the way he'd seen any Fae female.

"Your mind is somewhere else," Ren said and made to punch me in the gut. I blocked him just in time and countered, which he blocked, too.

"I'm tired," I said. "I had a rough night."

Lately, I'd been struggling to sleep. When I closed my eyes, I saw images, like thoughts, like memories. Like dreams. I didn't know what I saw—the flashes were so vivid. They came when I was almost asleep, and when I jerked awake, I couldn't remember what I'd seen.

"Really?" he asked and grinned. "Someone keeping you up?"

"Someone?" I asked with a laugh. "Yeah, sure. Dex and his routine of *never* sleeping after our training sessions."

"It's a tough routine, I'll admit," Ren said. "I thought you were made of better stuff than that."

His jab surprised me, but he laughed. He was still joking.

"I thought I was too fragile." I stuck my tongue out at him, and it was his turn to be surprised at my joke. But it was just a joke; we were messing with each other.

And it was *nice.* He was so handsome when he laughed and joked like that. Much more handsome than when he was so serious about everything, mourning the past and nervous about the future.

Ren lunged at me and tackled me. I rolled the way Dex had taught me so that I would end up on top of him. But he countered that, and we both ended up on our feet, facing off to each other.

"Nearly had you there," I said.

"But you didn't," he laughed.

I shook my head and stood upright. Without warning, Ren tackled me down, and this time, I couldn't counter in time. I ended up pinned to the ground with him on top of me, a smug grin on his face.

He leaned lower, his face close to mine, and the atmosphere shifted from playful to sensual in a heartbeat. I looked up to his lips. I wanted him to kiss me. Even if it confused the shit out of me because I never knew what he wanted. I wanted him to kiss me at least one more time. Then, I promised myself, I would stop thinking about him.

The arena shifted and changed, and the light had a distinct quality to it. I stared into Ren's eyes, but something crawled along my skin. Magic, dark and dangerous. Something was *wrong*.

"What's going on?" I asked.

"What do you—" He jumped up abruptly. "He's here," he said.

"Who?" I asked, pushing up, too.

"The hunter—the assassin."

Ren ran across the arena, and I followed him. We ran through the door that led to the palace and to the throne room.

The advisors were all huddled together, their dark robes adding to the serious tone.

Darkness had descended, making everything seem hazy and not quite in focus. It grew heavier and heavier, curled like black fog in the corners of the room.

"My weapons!" Ren shouted, and servants appeared seconds later with armor, a shield, a sword, and a helmet.

He was ready for battle in no time.

"Give me something to fight with!" I cried out.

"No." He spun around to face me as if he'd forgotten all about me. "Take her to her room."

"What?" I asked. "No!"

Nylah ran into the throne room, her eyes wide, chestnut hair streaming behind her like a cape.

"The dark magic is everywhere," she huffed breathlessly.

"I know. I'm taking care of it."

"Be careful," she said, and fear filled her eyes.

"I'll be fine," Ren assured her. He looked at the guards who'd circled me. "Take her away. Now."

The guards pointed for me to move toward the warrior quarters, but I wouldn't give in.

"No!" I shouted. "I'm fighting, too. Ren, let me fight."

He only shook his head.

Zita was among the warriors who circled me.

"Zita, please," I pleaded with her. "You know what I can do. You know we need all hands we can find for this."

She shook her head, torn between me and the King. But her loyalty lay with the King. We were all loyal to him.

"I'm sorry, Ellie," she said, and I believed she was.

When I still wouldn't move, the guards did what they needed to do. Two of the males I trained with grabbed me by the arms. I would have been able to fight them off if they hadn't used magic, but it pulsed through my body. I jerked involuntarily, like they'd electrocuted me, before I went limp. It took me less than a second to regain my strength and fight again.

I kicked and screamed, yelling at them to let me go. I threatened them with pain and anger, but they didn't listen. They carried me to my quarters as if I was nothing more than a kitten with my claws out.

Nylah followed behind me with Zita at her side. They both looked apologetic.

"Please, Nylah, make them understand!" I begged when I realized fighting wouldn't cut it.

"I agree with the King, Ellie," Nylah said. She looked guilty for saying it, but that didn't change her words.

"Are you kidding me right now? What did you train me for?" She had betrayed me! The realization made my stomach drop.

"I thought I had a friend in you!" I spat.

"Ellie...you can't even fight against these guards who are taking you to your room." I wanted to argue with her, but she was right. I was too upset to focus on blocking the power, too angry to think straight and fight.

The guards planted me on stiff legs in my room, and I glared at Nylah, who stood in the door, blocking my way. Zita stayed out of sight.

"So, that's what you reduced me to? A *human* with no skills, so I have to be babysat?"

Nylah shook her head. "You don't need a babysitter. I'll make sure you're safe."

"What?" I ran to the door, ready to take her out, too.

She mumbled a few words, and I felt a breath of magic.

When she turned and left with the guards at her side, I ran to the door to follow them. I wouldn't stay put, no matter how much Nylah trusted me to stay in my room! I didn't care what any of them said. I wanted to be there. I wanted to fight. I wanted to do what I'd trained to do.

I slammed into something hard. It was like a magical force field, keeping me from leaving my room.

I tried again, ran at the door and tried to force my way through the magic. But I couldn't get out.

When I rushed to my windows, they had the same magic keeping me from getting out of it. I was trapped in my room. No matter how well I could block magic, I couldn't make it go away—especially when it didn't come at me.

I let out a frustrated cry before I sank to the floor and leaned my head against the door.

Nylah hadn't left a babysitter with me because, with her magic, she didn't have to worry about anything. I couldn't get through. She was the High Priestess who moved in the Second Realm, close to the Goddess Terra.

Terra wouldn't help me escape from my room, either. I didn't even have to ask to know that.

I sat on the floor, furious. Then, my anger gave way to fear. I started getting worried about Ren. If the power had been that strong in the arena, what could this Conjurite do to him? Ren was powerful, but this was a different magic.

It was laced with death.

And it was terrifying.

I wanted to be there to help. I wanted to be there to protect him.

What if he didn't come back?

No, I couldn't think like that. I had to be sure that Ren was strong enough to win. And that Nylah would help him. Who was I kidding? I was just a human. I couldn't do enough to save either of them, no matter how much it bruised my ego.

I was small and useless, and I hated it.

I'd chosen to stay here and found there was more to life than just being alive. And now, after it all, I still wasn't enough to make a difference. I was worth no more here than I'd been as a barmaid. At least there, no one had had to look out for me. Here, I distracted Ren, Nylah, and Dex from doing their jobs because they were trying to protect me.

It was all backward.

The darkness pulsed around me, the strength renewed, and it poked and prodded the fear I barely had under control, threatening to break its restraints and set my fear free.

The sunlight fell through my open curtains, painting a line of fire on the carpet and shining in my eyes. I blinked them open and rolled onto my side before I pushed myself up.

My body was stiff. I'd slept on the floor. I'd fallen asleep in front of the door, waiting for someone to come get me out of the prison they'd created for me. I remembered trying to fight off the fear, trying to stand up against a power that didn't have to be right next to me to get to me.

When I stretched, my aching muscles complained, and my bones popped. I rolled my shoulders and walked to the bathroom. I showered and got dressed in fresh clothes before I tried to leave my room again.

This time, the magic was gone. I could leave my room without struggling.

I looked up and down the hallway that led to the warriors' rooms. No one was in sight. I'd overslept the time I usually had to train, and no one had fetched me.

Dex hadn't pulled me out of bed—or from the floor—by my feet and told me what a disappointment I was.

When I stepped into the mess hall, it was quiet. I picked up a piece of toast from a platter that had been left behind and nibbled on it as I walked through the palace.

Everything was quiet. Too quiet. I couldn't see a single servant, and it seemed like the palace was a shell, hiding secrets.

"Hello?" I called when I reached the throne room. "Anybody?"

Dex appeared from a side room.

"Ellie," he said. "You're here."

"Where else was I supposed to be?" I asked. "I couldn't be anywhere else, thanks to Nylah's spell."

Dex's face remained unchanged. I couldn't tell what he was thinking.

"Where's Ren?" I asked. "What happened with the fight?"

He hesitated before he chose his words carefully.

"The fight wasn't what it should have been. Ren was injured."

"What?" My stomach dropped to my shoes. "How badly is he hurt? Is he okay?"

"The healers are tending to him," Dex said.

That didn't sound good.

"What happened?"

He shook his head. "Dark magic isn't to be trifled with."

"But he's powerful," I countered. "Ren is one of the most powerful Fae ever to live, right? Isn't that what everyone says?"

"He's powerful, all right," Dex said. "But the dark magic..." He trailed off.

I stormed past him and down the hallway that led to the King's wing. I'd never been here, but I knew where it was.

When Nylah appeared in front of me, she looked panicked for a moment.

"Ellie," she said.

"You trapped me in my room, and then I'm the last to find out he's hurt?" I demanded. "I want to see him."

"He's with the healer, now," she said, shaking her head.

"You locked me up like a child last night," I replied. "You couldn't even talk to me and trust that I could help."

"It was for your own safety," she insisted. "It's what Ren ordered."

"And you think he was right?"

"We're friends, Ellie, but he's still my king. I can't just tell him no. He wanted to protect you. You should see it as a good thing."

Maybe she was right. But I struggled to see it that way when they'd kept me from the action for being too *fragile*, and then finding out like this that Ren had been hurt.

"I need to see him," I said in a softer voice. "Please. If I had been there, maybe he wouldn't have gotten hurt."

"Or you would have gotten hurt, too," Nylah said.

I shook my head. I didn't care. What if I could have changed things for him?

"It's bad, isn't it?" I asked dully. "If you won't let me see him."

I looked into Nylah's golden eyes, and they shimmered with unshed tears.

It *was* serious.

My heart constricted. My feelings for Ren were one-sided, but that didn't mean they weren't there. If something happened to him and we lost him...

The mere thought made my throat swell shut, and I couldn't breathe properly.

"I'll let you see him for a moment," Nylah finally said.

"Thank you," I said, relieved.

She opened the door to the King's room and talked to someone inside. It was back and forth for a bit, but then she looked at me and nodded.

"You only have a few minutes. He's not awake."

I swallowed hard, my stomach twisting into a knot of nerves. I walked into the room and looked around.

The healer who'd been with him had left through another door, and we were alone in the room. Me and Ren, without an audience.

"Ren?" I asked.

He didn't answer. He lay in bed with blankets tucked all around him, and he looked smaller than he should have. When I walked slowly toward him, I noticed how ashen his cheeks had become. His dark hair was pitch black against his pale skin, and his eyes were sunken. His cheeks were sallow, and he looked like he was barely alive. If it wasn't for the shallow rise and fall of his chest as he breathed—every breath seemingly a struggle—I would have thought he was dead already.

"Oh, Ren," I said, sitting down in the seat next to the bed. I took his hand. His skin was paper thin and cool to the touch. When I pressed my fingers against his wrist, his pulse fluttered lightly, like it was going to go out at any moment.

It hit me. Hard. Ren could *die*. He looked like he had to have been there already.

"You can't leave," I pleaded. "Not now. They all need you. Jasfin needs you. Who's going to lead them against Palgia if a war breaks out and you're not here?"

He didn't answer me. He just lay there, looking worse and worse by the minute.

"Where am I supposed to go if you go?" I asked. "I don't belong anywhere. I belong here. You gave me a home, one I'd never thought I could have. If you leave, it all falls apart, and then..." I squeezed my eyes shut, and tears rolled over my cheeks. "I don't want you to die. It's too soon. You still have so much to do as king. So many citizens to save...and you have me. I know it's not much, and that you don't care about me the way I care about you. More than you'll ever know. I'm too terrified to tell anyone. And I can't tell you. Not to your face—you're Fae, and I'm not. I'm just...me. And who needs that? You don't, I know you don't. But...I need *you*. And I know that's selfish to say, but I don't want you to go, because I don't know what I'd be without you. When I'm here, I have a purpose. I'm a warrior. Just hold on, okay? Just keep fighting. I'll be here when you wake up, and I'll stand behind you. I'll face anything that comes your way until the end of my days. Even if it's just as your warrior. Because I'd rather have that—I'd rather be with you just as your warrior—than not be with you at all."

I couldn't get the rest of my words out, but I'd said what I needed to say. I'd been carrying these feelings around for so long. It felt good to have voiced them, even if it had been nothing more than a shout into the void.

"Please," I whispered. "I won't bear it if you die."

The door opposite the bed opened, and an old male with a white beard and cream robes shuffled into the room. He had silver embellishments on his clothing, and he wore rings on all his fingers.

"I need to heal him, my lady," he said. "It's time for you to leave."

I nodded. I needed the healer to pull him through. I needed Ren to make it.

I walked to the door and let myself out of the room, fighting back the rest of my tears, swallowing hard to get rid of the lump in my throat.

"He's so sick," I whispered when Nylah appeared.

"He is," she agreed. Her face was serious, her eyes dark with concern. In them, I recognized my fear. It scared her he might die, too.

"Can't you do anything?" I asked. "You're the High Priestess. You're the one with the healing power. Why aren't you there, pulling him through? That's what you did for me."

She shook her head. "I've done all I can. The other healers are adding their magic to my own. Now, we wait to see if..."

It wasn't an answer. She couldn't finish her sentence, and I didn't want her to. I bowed my head and nodded, tears rolling over my cheeks yet again.

"Ellie," Nylah said, and I glanced up at her. "You haven't known him as long as we have, but that doesn't mean that he can't mean a lot to you. I know how much it hurts. I'm sorry."

"It's not your fault," I said.

"No, but I'm still sorry. And I'm sorry for what I did last night."

"He's your king. You had to obey," I said.

I hated it, but I understood it. All of it—that Ren had tried to keep me safe, that Nylah was loyal to him...and that this could be the end.

Nylah stepped forward and hugged me. The warmth that flowed from her enveloped me. Her magic warmed me from the inside, and I knew she was using magic to drive the sorrow away.

She just didn't know how deep it went because she didn't know how in love I was with Ren.

24

I fell back into a normal routine. I woke up early, ate, trained, showered and ate, and trained again. My heart wasn't in it. I was going through the motions, because I'd promised I would always be here and do what needed to be done to be a warrior for the King.

I was worried about him. Nylah told me he was doing better, but I couldn't see him again. He was unconscious most of the time, and the few times he was awake, Nylah didn't want anyone to bother him. He needed his rest.

A part of me was wilting, and I didn't know why. Was it because Ren had nearly died, and I hadn't been there to help him? Or was it because after it all, I'd finally poured my heart out to him, but he would never know?

I tried not to think about it too much.

When I came into my room a few days later, sweaty and tired after training hard with the warriors, I was at my end. I'd been through a hell of a lot in my life, having fought tooth and nail to survive since birth. I'd never felt like this, though. I'd never had to get out of my own way because I was dragging myself down.

I drew a bath and lay in salts and minerals until the water went cold before I climbed out. I dried my hair and wrapped the towel around my body to find clothes in my closet.

When I opened the bathroom door, Ren stood in my room.

"Oh, Goddess," I breathed. "You're here."

He nodded. He was tall and upright as always, albeit a little less broad than usual. He'd been through a lot. He'd fought to stay alive, and it showed.

I forgot I was in a towel and rushed to him. I stopped in front of him, keeping myself from grabbing him and holding on tight.

"You don't know how relieved I am."

"If it's anything like what I feel, I think I do," Ren said.

He smiled at me, and my stomach tightened.

"What happened?" I asked.

He shook his head. "It's not important."

"You nearly died," I said. "Of course it's important."

"It's not worth talking about."

I was getting frustrated. "After all that, you're going to leave me in the dark?"

"All what?" Ren asked.

"Why are you being such a pain in my ass? Do you have any idea how worried I was about you? Do you know what it was like waiting every day for them to tell me you were dead?" I bristled. "You don't get to stand here and tell me it's not important. Hell, Ren, this is a matter of—"

"I know," he said softly. "It's been rough on you."

"On all of us," I whispered.

"But I'm here. I didn't die. I'm okay."

I wanted to speak, but he shook his head and brushed his thumb across my lips.

"You can't do that," I said. But my voice was already breathy.

"Do what?"

"This...thing you do. Where you touch me, or kiss me, and then it's nothing. I can't do it, Ren. I can't..." I didn't know how to tell him I couldn't have my love be unreciprocated without telling him I was in love with him.

Ren's eyes locked on mine, and it was as if he looked into my soul.

His eyes were the color of the ocean, a deep blue that I could drown in if I wasn't careful.

That was exactly the problem.

Ren reached for me and ran his fingers through my hair. He leaned closer. I wanted to fight it. I wanted to step away, to tell him he had to back off if he wanted to let me keep my sanity at all. But I didn't. I couldn't. I wouldn't stop him.

He closed the distance between us and kissed me. It was urgent, more serious than what it had been before. Before, we'd worked on borrowed time. At any moment, something would interrupt us. This time, there was nothing to bother us. My bedroom door was closed, and it was just the two of us.

And he kissed me like there was no tomorrow.

Goddess, there almost hadn't been.

Ren pulled me closer to him so that our bodies were pressed together, and I was suddenly very aware that I was just in a towel.

"I have to get dressed," I whispered.

Ren shook his head. "Don't," he murmured against my lips.

His hand slid from my cheek into my neck and then my bare shoulders. He thumbed my collarbone before he traced the skin just above the edge of my towel. He moved his hips and ground his erection against me. His need for me was evident, and it echoed my own.

"Ren," I whispered, but he reached for the towel where I'd tucked it around my chest. He looked into my eyes, a question.

I wouldn't stop him.

When he undid the towel, it fell to the floor, and I stood before him, naked.

He glanced down, his eyes roaming my body, and I let him look at me. After weeks of training, my body had become fit, my muscles lean and hard. Now that I was eating regular, hearty meals, I also had curves that had never been there before. Ren reached for me, and when his fingertips touched my body, electricity flowed through my veins.

He traced the scars that wrapped around my arms, the cuts that had become thick ridges of skin on my back. He took in all of me. I'd been abused a lot of times. I wasn't ashamed of my scars—they were proof that I was stronger than what had happened to me. They were proof that I'd survived.

When Ren looked me in the eye, his gaze was filled with wonder and lust, and he kissed me again. His hands found my breasts, and he kneaded and massaged them. He tweaked my erect nipples, and I moaned as his attention made me hot for him. Wetness pooled at my center the more he touched me, and I wanted him.

I wanted all of him.

Ren gently guided me toward the bed and urged me to sit down. He pushed me backward, and he started planting kisses on my chest, my abdomen, moving down toward my hips. When he reached my pubic bone, my legs fell open for him, and I gasped.

I couldn't believe this was happening. It was surreal. I'd fantasized about him doing this so many times, and now he was here, doing it.

When he closed his mouth over my center, I stopped thinking altogether. I got lost in the pleasure as he flicked his tongue back and forth over my clit. I moaned and pushed my hands into his dark hair. He glanced up at me, and his eyes were dark, his pupils so dilated I could barely see the icy blue around them.

He looked primal, and his need reflected my own.

He flicked his tongue faster, alternating it with sucking on my clit, and I closed my eyes, letting the sensation sweep me up.

When I was on the edge of an orgasm, Ren slid two fingers into me. I cried out at the change of pace and the new sensation of his fingers inside of me.

He pumped them in and out, stroking my walls, making me ache to feel him inside of me. I wanted Ren between my legs, thrusting his cock into me. I wanted his lips against mine while he did, our breathing mixed and our hearts beating as one.

Ren continued to move his fingers in a rhythmic pace while he sucked my clit. Painfully slow, he pushed me closer and closer to the edge. Every time I thought I would topple over, he changed tactics on me, leaving me aching for more, teased and frustrated. He was drawing it out, and he seemed to enjoy what it was doing to me.

"Please," I moaned, curling on the bed when I was ready to come undone at the seams, but he'd stopped me from doing so yet again.

He chuckled, his mouth against my center, and the vibrations shocked through my body.

Ren sucked on my clit again and moved his fingers. He kept the same rhythm with his mouth as he did with his fingers, and slowly, he picked up speed. The pleasure that had been just beneath the surface exploded and washed over me. I cried out, closed my thighs around his head, and let the orgasm crash down on me again and again.

It was intense, incredible, and I moaned and groaned as I squirmed and writhed on the bed.

When I came down from my sexual high, I lay on the bed, panting. I looked down at Ren, who smiled at me, looking more than satisfied.

"Let me please you," I said, out of breath.

Ren shook his head and took my hand. He pulled me up, so we both stood. Ren wrapped his arms around me, pressing his body to mine, and kissed me.

"This was just about giving you pleasure. It isn't about me."

"But I want to please you," I said.

Ren just kissed me again. He bent down and reached for the towel that still lay on the floor where he'd dropped it and handed it to me.

"I just wanted to let you know I'm okay," he said.

I tucked the towel against my chest.

"Okay," I replied in a small voice. He kissed me again before he walked to the door.

"Sleep well, Ellie."

I was suddenly exhausted. I still had to go to dinner in the mess hall, but I wanted to sink back onto my pillows and bathe in the aftermath of the orgasm Ren had just given me.

25

I lay on my bed with Ren, laughing at something he'd said. He was so relaxed when he was away from the demands of his palace life. He talked about his past without wincing at the recent death of his father, and being around him was a pleasure.

I'd only seen glimpses of the male he could be when royal responsibility didn't weigh him down. But the more time we spent together, the more I saw a side of him I could resonate with.

There was no reason we could relate to each other, him and I. Ren was the most powerful king to ever rule Jasfin. I was just a human. We had nothing in common; not where we had come from, not where we were going, and not who we were.

And yet, being with Ren was...right.

"Do you want to know what I think?" I asked.

"Sure," Ren said. "Tell me what you think."

He played with my hand, our fingers interlinking, twisting around each other. We were touching, even though we lay apart from each other on the bed.

"I think..." I glanced up at him and stopped in the middle of my sentence. "What's wrong?"

"What are you talking about?" he asked.

"Your eyes..."

His usually ice-blue eyes had turned red, the color of embers when the fire had died out. When I stared into them, I saw pits of darkness. I felt like I stood on the edge when I looked at him, like I was going to topple over.

And once that happened, I was going to fall forever...

I snapped my head around and squeezed my eyes shut.

"What's the matter, Eleanor?" Ren asked. "Scared of the monsters under your bed?"

He gripped my shoulders and wrenched me around, and when I opened my eyes, Ren wasn't in front of me anymore. Instead, it was a monster, with eyes like the burning pits of hell and skin like that of a lizard or a snake. The dark hair on his head was tangled and stuck up in tufts.

I jerked awake, breathing hard. I struggled to catch my breath. It felt like my chest was going to implode. I gulped air, but my body wouldn't cooperate.

Something wasn't right.

I tried to wriggle free of the nightmare that held onto me with claws—the same claws that had dug into my shoulders when the monster had grabbed me.

That hadn't been Ren. It had been exactly what I'd seen—a monster.

I became aware of my quarters, of my bedroom, and I wasn't alone.

Something was here with me, and with it came the darkness that could force itself into beings, darkness that took over.

"Who's there?" I asked.

A deep voice chuckled, and I curled in fear.

"You're sharp for a human," the voice said, and a shadow stepped from the darkness. The terror that came with his every movement was so much stronger than anything I felt. In a dream or otherwise. This was dark magic.

And this male, standing in front of me...

"You're a Conjurite," I gasped in horror.

He chuckled, and the sound of it rubbed up against my skin, slick and warm, like spit. I rubbed my arms, trying to get rid of the feel of the sound.

"You're not stupid, I'll give you that. Usually, you humans are so oblivious it's fucking pathetic. But you...you're different. Pity I'll have to kill you."

"Why would you want to do that?" I asked.

Slowly, I climbed out of bed. The fear was still there, ever-present, coiled in the pit of my stomach. But I was thinking clearly. The worst was wearing off. This was what my training was for—so that I could think straight when my usual response would have been fight-or-flight. Or freeze, in this case.

"I don't *want* to do it," the shadow said. "But these are my orders. I'm sure you understand how it works when you're told to do something, and you've pledged your loyalty, you do what you need to do."

I needed to keep him talking. As long as he was talking—and the bad guys just *loved* to monologue—I could ready myself for a fight.

"Who sent you?" I demanded.

The shadow laughed again. "I know what you're doing. You're trying to distract me. You're banking on the fact that I love the sound of my own voice. But you see...I don't fall for parlor tricks."

"And yet, you hide away in the darkness, so no one can see who you are. Talk about a parlor trick," I said.

He hesitated for a moment. I could almost feel him draw his breath.

"Fine," he said, sounding pissed. He stepped forward and into the light of the moon that fell through the window.

Darkness still danced at the edge of my vision, his magic painfully clear. This dark magic wasn't power I could block—not the way I had to, to save my life. This hunter had nearly killed Ren, the most powerful Fae of all.

Fear bloomed in the pit of my stomach again, escaping from the tight coil I tried to keep it wound up in. I forced myself to breathe, to think straight. Panicking wouldn't help. It would only get me killed.

When he stood in the moonlight, I frowned.

That stature, that face...

I flashed back on a reflection in the metal siding of an arena, a fight with a monster that felt like it had taken place ages ago.

"Zander?" I gasped.

That took him aback. He didn't expect me to know who he was.

"You killed King Rainier's father," I added, shocked that it was him and suddenly furious at what he'd done to Ren. When I'd been brought to the palace originally, I had been in this Fae's body.

"Yeah, well, what did I tell you about loyalty?"

This time, he didn't wait for me to answer or to ask more questions that would stall for time. He'd been in control all this time. He lunged at me—an attack that came with a burst of magic so powerful it took my breath away. I felt like I was in a furnace, with heat dancing on my skin. I was sure it would burn off my clothes, singe all the hair on my head, leave me naked and raw and terrified.

I blocked what I could, the way Nylah had taught me. And for a moment, a cool breeze put out the fire on my skin, and I could take a deep breath.

Zander faltered for just a moment. He hadn't expected me to block his power. I'd shocked him a second time.

I was just as surprised. I hadn't thought I could do anything, either.

"It's a curse, Eleanor," he said.

"What is?" I asked.

He attacked before he answered, and I blocked the blow. He was stronger than I was, but I held up my end, until he brought his magic out to play. The blazing heat came with a renewed strength, and I screamed. I couldn't fight it this time, and I thought it was going to consume me. My vision blurred and became black, and it was just a matter of time before the fire and the darkness—such a strange combination—would consume me.

The door burst open, and a fresh wave of power pushed into the room. Dex stood there, a snarl on his face. Nylah was with him, driving the magic. It was too much for Zander to face them and me.

He turned, ran to the window, and in a flash, he was gone.

"After him!" Dex shouted, and warriors barged into my room.

Six warriors went out the window after him. Two remained, keeping watch in case he came back this way. I heard more shouts from outside my window, where warriors were searching.

"He's gone," I said.

"Are you okay?" Nylah asked, rushing to me.

Dex cursed under his breath and ran out of the room, ready to continue the search, but they wouldn't find anything.

"It was him," I said, trembling.

"The hunter," Nylah said, nodding.

"Not just the hunter, it was Zander."

Her eyes widened. "Are you sure?"

I nodded. "I've been in his body. There was no doubt about it."

Nylah shook her head. "We need to tell Dex. If Zander is behind the attacks, this is bigger than just the assassination of the King."

I couldn't think anymore. I was trembling with shock and the aftermath of the adrenaline pumping through my veins, and I felt drained and weak.

"Come, we need to get you to bed."

Nylah helped me up and tucked me into bed the way I imagined a mother would. She sat on the edge of the bed, holding my hand, and I felt a cool breeze wash over me. She was using her magic to soothe me, to heal what he'd damaged. I wasn't sure what damage had been done. I didn't know what scope the dark magic had and how it could hurt me. I'd seen what Ren had looked like after the Conjurite—who I now knew was Zander—had attacked him.

But I didn't feel like death warmed up.

At least...I didn't think so.

Dex returned. He looked grim.

"He got away," he mumbled. "But we'll get him. Now that we know..." He looked at me. "The King wants to see you."

I frowned. "Me?"

Dex nodded.

"You should go," Nylah said. "You'll be safe."

I was still scared. But Dex would be with me, and when I left my room, warriors surrounded me like I was of royal blood myself and needed to be protected.

Ren was awake and pacing in his room when we arrived. When he saw me, he looked at Dex.

"Thank you," he said with gratitude in his voice.

Dex nodded curtly and barked an order to his warriors, who left.

I was alone with Ren.

He came to me and wrapped his arms around me, pulling me tightly against him.

"I'm so glad you're okay. I can't believe he was in your room."

"What was he after?" I asked.

"He wanted to kill you," Ren said, and his voice trembled. "I don't know what I would have done."

I tried to figure out how that was possible. How could he be after me? He'd tried to kill the King. That was what he was in Jasfin for. Wasn't it?

Ren planted kisses all over my face.

"I don't know what I would have done if he'd hurt you. After what he did to me..."

He'd never talked to me about what had happened. I wanted to know, but I didn't want to think about it tonight. I was exhausted after what had occurred.

"Come," Ren said, leading me to his bed.

He pulled me onto the mattress with him and curled me tightly against him. He stroked my hair. He wanted me near him to keep me safe. He was doting on me. He was caring for me. He was relieved I was still okay.

I didn't know why that made me feel so much better. Knowing that Ren cared as much as he did made me feel refreshed. I would be there for him, like I'd promised when he'd been so close to death. I would be there for him, no matter what, because I cared about him in a way I'd never cared about anyone.

But if he felt that way about me, too—if he returned my affection —it changed everything. It made what I felt for him feel like less of a burden.

"I don't know what's happening between us," I whispered when Ren showered me with kisses again.

"I don't know, either," he admitted. "All I know is that I need to keep you close to me. When I heard he was here, that he'd made his way into the palace, into your *room*..." The fear in his eyes told me more than Ren could with words.

I was the one to kiss him. I swallowed his words, the rest of what he wanted to say. No more fear. No more worry. No more panic. We were both okay. We were alive and well.

And we were together.

Ren stopped trying to explain to me what he felt, and he kissed me back. The kiss was urgent, and I poured everything I felt for him into it. With our lips locked, I felt what I wanted to feel for Ren without guilt.

His large hands roamed my body, and despite my new strength and sculpted body, he made me feel feminine and delicate. He gyrated his hips against mine, grinding against my hipbone, and I felt his erection. He wanted me.

And I wanted him. I *ached* for him. I wanted him to fill me up. I wanted him to take every inch of me, and I wanted to do the same with him, so that we could be closer than we already were.

Ren kissed a line down my neck, leaving a trail of fire in his wake. His hands found their way under the t-shirt I slept in, and they were hot on my skin, branding me. I gasped when he pushed my shirt up and cried out when he sucked my left nipple into his mouth.

Ren worshiped my body, kissing and licking and sucking, alternating between my breasts. He made me feel like I was a goddess, beautiful, ethereal, and when I was with him, I felt like I could be his equal.

When he moved down my body, I pulled my large t-shirt over my head, and I was naked, save for my socks. Ren kissed his way down my body, but this time, I wanted to be the one to please him.

I put my hand on his cheek and gently led him to come back up to my mouth so that I could kiss him. With our lips locked, I pulled up his shirt and traced the individual muscle groups of his perfectly muscular torso. His muscles rippled under his skin when he moved, his large arms wrapping around me.

I groaned and kissed his light skin, moving down his body. He was incredibly well built, chiseled by the angels themselves and sent back here.

I reached the waistband of his pants and slowly peeled it over his hips. His cock sprung free, hard and ready, and I marveled at it for a moment. His size was impressive, silky-smooth skin stretching over his thick shaft, silk over steel.

When I wrapped my fingers around him, he hissed through his teeth. I started pumping my hand up and down, and he groaned, pushing his hands into my hair. He held on tight, and I pumped my hand faster and faster.

I wanted more.

I wanted to taste him.

I lowered my head and sucked the tip into my mouth. Ren groaned and grabbed tightly onto my hair. The sensation only made me shiver and want him more. I got wetter as I touched him and licked him and sucked him.

I bobbed my head up and down, stroking him in and out of my mouth. He was too big for me to take far into my mouth, but I did what I could, and judging by the moans Ren made, it was more than enough.

He pulled back, suddenly, and I glanced up at him.

"Not yet," he growled. "I don't want to finish yet."

He pulled me up and kissed me, his tongue in my mouth and hands roaming my naked body. My breasts were against his naked chest, and his thick flesh lay against my stomach, scalding hot.

Ren flipped me over in one easy gesture, and I lay on my back, looking up at him.

"I've waited too long for this," he growled and positioned himself between my legs.

If he only knew.

His tip pushed against my entrance, and I held my breath and moaned when he slid into me. His size was a challenge, but he moved slowly and allowed me to adjust.

When he was buried inside of me, I trembled around him.

"You're...beautiful," he murmured, kissing me between words.

He started moving, and I gasped and moaned as he pulled back until only the tip was buried inside me. He slid back in, and I yelped as I adjusted to his size once more. With every stroke, my body became more and more accustomed to his size, and the almost-pain I'd been teetering on disappeared, replaced by nothing but sheer pleasure.

Ren started rocking harder and faster. He slid in and out of me, bucking his hips, and I let it all go. I closed my eyes and got lost in the sensation. His large, powerful body hovered over mine. He held himself up enough not to crush me, and I was very aware of how powerful he was.

He could snap me like a twig, but the way he handled me was with the utmost care.

Ren would never hurt me.

I stopped thinking about how incredible he was, how much I cared for him, and how perfect it was that this was finally happening after nights and nights of dreaming about him. I only focused on how good it felt.

I moaned with every stroke, and Ren grunted and groaned along with me.

I hadn't orgasmed yet, but the pleasure built in my core, slowly becoming bigger and bigger. Ren pumped harder, and that door between us opened. I knew what he was thinking. I knew what he was feeling. And I found his thoughts and emotions only an echo of my own. We were wrapped up in each other, we'd become one, so much that I didn't know where I ended and he began.

The pleasure kept building, and when it was so powerful I couldn't hold back anymore, I came undone at the seams.

I cried out as the orgasm ripped through me, starting at my core and flooding my body. I curled on the bed, back arched, and let out a cry as I felt like I was going to fracture and burst into a million particles of light.

I felt Ren's pleasure building and knew he was going to orgasm, too, before he did. He buried himself within me, as deep as he would go, and when he released inside of me, my wave of pleasure was still rolling. The orgasm was incredible, and it rocked through me, pulling me apart. I had only Ren to keep me together.

And that door between us shattered, so that we couldn't be blocked off between each other again.

"Oh, Ellie," Ren gasped, and light filled the room.

I blinked, not sure what was happening. I struggled to focus on what was going on with the pleasure washing through me over and over, as if there was no end.

Finally, after it felt like eternity that I was held at the pinnacle of absolute pleasure, I came down from the pure bliss.

Ren stared at me in awe. He touched me like I would disappear before his eyes if he blinked too hard. I frowned and lifted my hand to touch his face.

That was when I saw it. My skin was glowing. It shimmered and glowed as if it was a source of energy and light. I turned my hand over and over, looking at my skin, blinking, trying to understand what I saw.

"What's going on?" I asked.

"I don't know," Ren admitted. "But you're incredible."

I wanted to fear what I saw. I wanted to panic, but I couldn't. The light was soothing, and Ren wasn't scared. I felt it as if I was him and he was me—as if we had a bond, a direct line. He was in awe of me, staring at me in wonder and amazement.

Slowly, as the sexual pleasure faded, so did the glowing sensation.

Until I was nothing more than Ellie, a human, lying in a puddle of sweat in the middle of the Fae King's bed.

26

I lay in bed next to Ren. The lights were off, and the moonlight sufficed to see each other by. He played with my hands, just like I'd dreamed before everything had gone wrong.

But he didn't turn into a monster, and he didn't keep his distance. He lay tightly against me, his body curled around mine like a question mark.

"I don't know what it means," I said. "Have you ever seen that before?"

Ren shook his head. "No. I've been alive a long time, and I've seen a lot of power and a lot of Fae, but nothing like that. Nothing that glowed with an ethereal surge of...I don't know what it was."

I nodded. I wasn't sure if I should fear what had happened. A part of me still wanted to panic, but I felt strangely calm, and it overtook everything else I felt.

Except for this incredible bond I felt with Ren.

But that made little sense, didn't it? Fae and humans couldn't bond. We weren't of the same species.

Besides, I'd read all about the bonding and mating and rituals that went with it, and I wasn't sure it was real. People fell back on a lot of legends—it was like that with any culture. Stories were told from one generation to the next, and they got bigger in the retelling. They became wilder.

I couldn't be connected to Ren the way I thought I was.

Could I?

"Do you think we should be worried?" I asked.

Ren shook his head. "It didn't hurt, right?"

I shook my head. "I didn't even realize it."

"I don't think we should be worried. But I want to know what it means. We'll ask Nylah about it and see what she has to say. Maybe there's something in the history books..."

Ren's voice tapered off, and I knew he was thinking what I was thinking. We both knew the Fae history. He'd grown up with it, and I'd studied it extensively the last while to understand the world I was living in now.

And not once had anything like this popped up.

Ren kissed my naked shoulder. "I'm just glad you're safe. And that you're here," he said.

Through the connection we shared, I felt a wash of affection, and it warmed me. He meant exactly what he said.

Did he feel it, too?

I was too scared to ask. What if it was all just infatuation? What if it was one-sided? What if I believed in some fairy tale that didn't exist, and he didn't feel a thing?

I wanted to wait until he mentioned it before I would talk about it. I didn't know if it was real, or if it was even possible.

Ren would know if he felt it. He would mention it. I was sure he would. A mate bond—if it existed—wasn't to be taken lightly. At least, not according to what I'd read.

But it wasn't something that the Fae chased after the way they used to anymore, either. So...how important—and how real—could it be?

"Your mind is going to drive you crazy," Ren said.

I blinked at him. "What do you mean?"

"I can almost see the cogs turning."

I wanted to know if he *felt* it, too, but he didn't say as much.

I snuggled further into the blankets. "I just have to switch off after a crazy night."

"It's a good idea to get some sleep," Ren said.

I waited for him to ask me to go back to my room. He didn't. Instead, he threw an arm over me and pulled me closer. Soon, his breathing became heavier, and he fell asleep. A peaceful slumber dragged me under, too.

When I woke up, Ren was gone. I was alone in his bed, still naked, and I felt vulnerable and shy. The sun streamed through the windows.

Damn it! I'd overslept. *Again.*

I jumped up and wrapped one of Ren's robes around my body. I wouldn't run through the palace in the oversized t-shirt—and nothing else—I'd worn when I got here. Last night, it had seemed okay in the darkness, but in the bright light of day, it was far too much like a walk of shame.

Although I felt no shame or regret about sleeping with Ren.

Just confusion.

I poked my head out of his room and looked right into Nylah's golden eyes.

She smirked at me.

"Morning," I said, rubbing my forehead with my fingertips. I wanted to blurt out that this wasn't what it looked like, but it was exactly what it looked like. Besides, she was my friend. I had no reason to be embarrassed about sleeping with Ren.

"I was just about to come get you," she said. "Did you sleep well?"

I nodded.

"Dex told me to let you know after a rough night last night, you're granted the day off."

I relaxed. I wasn't in trouble for missing training, at least.

It *had* been a rough night. When I thought about what Ren and I had done, I blushed.

Nylah and I walked in silence to my quarters. She told me she would wait while I showered and changed, and when I was ready, we walked to the cathedral.

"Ren told me about your glowing," Nylah said.

I glanced at her and blushed. "Did he tell you how and when it happened?"

She nodded. "It's not a secret that he's very fond of you, Ellie. You shouldn't be shy about it. If the King chooses you, it's a great honor."

She was so solemn about it. But then her face split into a smile. "Was it amazing?"

I giggled and nodded. "He's something else."

Nylah giggled, too. "I'm glad it's you, rather than that bitch."

I smiled. So was I.

We walked into the cathedral and finally settled on the couches in front of the fireplace. Nylah watched the fire dance. The fireplace was perpetually lit, making interesting shadows along the gothic arched ceilings.

"All of this is so unfamiliar," Nylah said. She furrowed her brow. "I feel like I should know the answers, but I'm completely out of my depth."

"You haven't ever heard of anything like this?" I asked.

She shook her head. "I'm sorry to say I have not. In all my years as a high priestess, it should be something I might have come across, or read about. Or...something."

She furrowed her brows. It was clear she felt like she *should* have known, and she was beating herself up about it.

"Things happen sometimes that we can't explain," I tried. "Maybe it was nothing."

Nylah shook her head. "It wasn't nothing. This doesn't happen— not even to Fae. And, you're a human."

She was right. It didn't happen to humans, either. Definitely not.

Everything had been so different since the day I'd arrived here. I perpetually felt like I was in over my head. Not only the Fae customs, the rituals, and all the magic they were used to seeing around them every day, but the history that I read, too. The stories that they grew up with as fact that seemed almost like a fantasy to me.

"Why don't I brew us some tea?" I asked.

Nylah nodded, staring into the flames. I stood and walked to the kitchenette that was next to her living room, where I put on a kettle to boil. I waited for the water, prepared two cups, and chose from one of the many pots of spiced tea.

When the hot cups of tea were ready, I carried them out to the living room on a tray and set them down on the low coffee table.

"Thank you," Nylah said when I handed her a cup.

I sat down, not touching mine yet.

Nylah sipped her tea, her eyes closed. When she opened them, she had a strange, otherworldly air to her.

"She won't tell me," she said in a soft voice.

"Who?"

"Terra. I asked her. I called on her when you were in the kitchen, asking her to give me answers that would explain what was going on. But...I got little. She wouldn't talk to me. No visions."

While she'd talked, I'd reached for my teacup. My hand was outstretched, but far from the cup, when it fell over, as if I'd touched it.

"Oh, no!" I cried out.

I felt it against my fingertips, felt the hot porcelain and felt my hand push it over. How was this possible? I was more than a foot away from it.

The hot tea spilled across the coffee table. I reached out with both hands, standing to pick up the cup. I held out my hands, and as I watched, the tea dried up. No, that wasn't it.

It flowed back into the cup that lay on its side. And then the cup righted itself.

Nylah and I both stared at the teacup, which looked like nothing had happened. The coffee table was dry. The tea looked untouched.

"What was that?" I asked, panicked.

"Magic," Nylah breathed.

"Was it you?"

She shook her head and looked at me with wide eyes. "No, Ellie. That was you."

"That's not possible," I said. I rubbed my hands on my thighs like I could get rid of whatever I'd just experienced. "I can't do magic."

"I don't agree with you," Nylah said. Her shock was turning into surprise, and a smile danced around her lips, tugging at the corners of her mouth. "This is what I asked for."

"What?" I was freaking out.

Too much was happening. Too much was unknown—all at once.

"I asked the Goddess to show me what was going on, and she wouldn't talk to me. But she's *showing* us, Ellie. Here."

She held out her hands. Without hesitation, I grabbed them. If she could fix whatever was going on, I wouldn't waste another minute.

Nylah looked at my hands as she held them, but I knew she was concentrating on what she felt, not what she saw. When she looked up at me, her eyes were filled with new knowledge, with a certainty that scared me.

"This is Fae magic, Ellie," she said.

"How can it be?" I asked. "Did the hunter do something to me?"

Or had it been Ren, because we'd slept together? I didn't verbalize that part. Nylah didn't seem concerned about it, but I still wasn't sure what to make of it.

Nylah shook her head. "Fae can't bestow magic on others, Ellie. That's not how it works. We are born with it, we wield it. Some are more powerful than others. But we can't give it to others. If you have Fae magic, then it's all yours."

I shook my head again and again. "This doesn't make sense."

"No, it doesn't." Nylah frowned, focusing on what she felt again. I watched her turn her concentration inward. "There's something else. Power that I don't understand."

"What do you mean?"

"I've never felt this kind of magic before. There's something about you..."

She let go of my hands and folded hers in her lap. She looked up at me, her face a mixture of expressions.

"We'll find out what's going on, Ellie. I promise. And none of this is bad, okay? The magic I sense in you, although unfamiliar, isn't evil."

I let out a breath I hadn't known I'd been holding. A part of me had wondered if this had been because of Zander and what he'd done. Even when Nylah had said they couldn't transfer magic.

"What am I?" I asked in a thin voice.

Nylah shook her head. "I don't know. That's what we're going to find out. But there is one thing I know—you're not fully human."

27

I struggled to wrap my mind around what was happening. My whole life had changed, but it was easy enough to get used to a new routine, to get fit and eat right and do all the things that made me ready for battle.

I'd still been human. I'd still been Ellie. I'd been myself.

But now, everything was changing. It wasn't just my home and my routine and where I belonged. Suddenly, I wasn't who I'd thought I was all this time.

And it was terrifying.

Nylah was set on figuring it out. She spent the next two days poring over books, locked up in her cathedral, going over everything she could find.

She found nothing.

I tried to do research of my own, but the palace library was filled with fiction rather than history books and books about magic and spells. Normally, I'd be okay with that—thankful, even. But right now, I needed some help.

My own books were no aid—the warriors had training manuals and historic accounts of wars won more than anything else on their shelves.

Nylah called for me on the third day. She looked thin and exhausted.

"I've been trying to find answers, but I have nothing for you, Ellie," she said. Her voice was apologetic.

"It's okay," I said.

"It's not." She shook her head. "I'm determined to find out what this is. I want to do a few rituals and spells, if that's okay with you. It's a bit more intense than the hand-holding we've done before, but I don't know how else to do it."

"Will it hurt?" I asked.

"Not at all. It's just different from what you've seen before."

I nodded. "Okay." I wanted her to find out what was going on with me.

Since I'd found out I had a bit of magic, I'd been too scared to use it. I'd been careful with everything I touched, but it hadn't shown up again. When I'd trained with Dex and the other warriors, I'd been myself.

Nylah beckoned for me to follow her through a door I'd never noticed before. The wood was so old, it had slivered with time, and when we stepped in, the room was dark. Candles sprang to light as we walked in. They were packed all over the room, on surfaces, on the floor, in chandeliers against the wall, and hanging from the ceiling. Dried wax littered the floor where it had dripped, and it looked like it had been here for centuries. The candles had melted down, standing on bases thick with wax, the bases of candles that had burned down before.

In the middle of the room stood a low stool with a pillow on top.

"Kneel there," Nylah said. "Close your eyes, and don't worry. I'll do the rest."

I did as she asked. Although she'd said not to worry, I tasted my heart in my throat. The idea of a ritual scared me.

Nylah started packing candles all around me, creating an intricate design I couldn't make out. She walked a few steps in certain directions, counting them off before muttering words in a language I didn't understand.

Eventually, so many candles surrounded me, if I moved in any direction, I would catch fire.

She mumbled under her breath. A breeze picked up in the room, making the flames dance on their wicks, causing shadows to flicker on the walls. The more Nylah mumbled, the more the wind blew, and the candles threatened to go out. But they didn't. We were surrounded by light.

Suddenly, we weren't alone in the room. A warm burst of energy joined us, another presence. I shivered. I was hyper-aware, feeling this *being* and the power that came with it. It was warm water pouring over my body.

It was only there for a moment before it disappeared again.

I watched as Nylah's face changed. She took on a surreal expression. Her skin became almost translucent, and it was clear she wasn't quite with me anymore.

She continued to mumble, and her face went through an array of emotions as she had what I assumed was a conversation with the Goddess Terra.

Finally, Nylah opened her eyes and looked right at me. The golden hue of her eyes glowed as if they were jewels, set alight by some divine inner flame.

"A human born with the light—" she started in a strange voice, but darkness swirled into the room and cut her off. The candles went out. One by one, as if they were being snuffed out by something moving past them.

I looked away from her, breaking eye contact, and suddenly, the shadows were everywhere. Darkness wrapped itself around me, and the Conjurite magic was so powerful, I couldn't breathe. With the last candles out and no windows in the room, we plunged into blackness.

It wrapped tighter and tighter around me. My ears started ringing, and it felt like my blood vessels were going to burst. My head pounded.

"Nylah," I croaked.

I couldn't see her. Couldn't fight back. Couldn't move.

"Ellie!" I heard her scream.

But the darkness won out, and I sank into oblivion.

28

I came to, lying on a cold hard stone. I shivered but kept my eyes closed. I listened to my surroundings. A dripping faucet was somewhere in the distance, and howling of the wind around corners filled my ears.

When I heard nothing else, I opened my eyes. The dim lighting was enough to pierce my skull with a stabbing headache, and I groaned. I clutched my head and curled into a ball on the stone, trying to breathe through the pain.

Slowly, it subsided enough that I could bear it, and I pushed up.

I looked around. I was in a cell with a stone floor and walls with nothing but a pile of rags in the corner. A window close to the ceiling was protected with metal bars, far too high for me to reach to look out of. Toward the front of the cell, there was a metal door with nothing more than a narrow slot carved in the center, which I assumed food could be passed through.

Where was I? How had I gotten here?

This situation was reminiscent of how I'd come to the palace. I prayed to the Goddess that I wasn't about to face another beast.

I shivered and rubbed my arms, trying to remember what had

happened. When I tried to think, the stabbing headache returned, and I groaned, trying to find memories around it.

Dimly, I flashed on Nylah, mumbling.

Candles in a dark room.

A human born with the light...

Then, dark magic had snuffed out all the light.

Now I was here, in a prison cell.

I shook my head and regretted it immediately. I'd been taken; I was sure of it. I didn't know why. I didn't know what I was or what I was capable of. But someone had to know something, or I wouldn't have been here.

Right? It was the only reasoning that made sense.

I pushed myself up. My body was stronger than I thought it would be. How long had I been out for? The light that fell through the little window against the ceiling let in enough light that I knew it was daytime, but that was all I could figure out.

"Hello?" I called, walking to the slot in the door.

No answer.

I peeked out but saw no one—not a guard, no other doors, no other prisoners.

"Is anybody there?" I called again.

I touched the door, pushed against it. There was no handle on the inside. I shoved it harder, threw my body weight against it. But the impact made my head ache all over again, and I was dizzy.

"I don't belong here!" I shouted.

The déjà vu was too much to bear.

I raised my hands and studied them. I touched my hair and ran the red locks through my fingers.

At least I was still myself. There was no spell, no disguise.

I turned and walked to the pile of rags and sat down. This was what I'd been used to sleeping on, once upon a time. But now it was hard and unforgiving. I pulled one rag up and wrapped it around my shoulders against the cold. I leaned my head back against the cold stone and closed my eyes to stop my head from throbbing so much.

Ren, my heart cried out. I wished he was here, or that I was with him. I was so alone. My heart was breaking. I'd dealt with a lot, and I'd been strong, but I was close to becoming undone.

I don't know where I am. I don't know if I can do this. I'm only so strong, and I'm just a human. Ren, where are you?

Tears burned my eyes.

Ellie, he answered, and my eyes shot open.

"Ren?" I asked out loud.

But his voice was in my head. Just like mine had been.

What's happening? I asked. How was this possible? How could I hear him?

We're connected, Ellie, he answered. *I can sense you. I can* feel *you. Are you hurt?*

I shook my head, but he couldn't see me. *Not physically. But I...I'm scared.*

I hadn't wanted to admit to it, but I couldn't stop myself from telling him. If anyone understood me, it was him. We were connected, and he knew my mind, he knew my heart.

Stay strong, he said. *I'm coming to get you.*

How do you know where I am? A spark of hope ignited inside me, but the terror was bigger than anything. It had to do with the Conjurite magic. It had to be. The terror had been overwhelming in my room the night Zander had attacked me, too. It was part of the evil in the Conjurite magic. It was a telltale sign.

I'll find you, Ren said fiercely, and I put my trust in him. I needed him. I wished I was back at the palace, in my quarters, or training in the arena. Or eating with the other warriors. Or...something. Anything other than *this*.

I tried to reach out to Ren, but our momentary connection was lost, and I was all alone again. Tears rolled over my cheeks, but I wiped them away, angry with myself for being so weak.

How much had I endured in my life? I'd been through abuse, I'd dealt with pain, I'd handled it all and come out the other side. I'd looked after myself with no one there to help me. I'd ended up at the palace as an *asset*. I was better than this.

Stronger than this.

I wouldn't let a cell get me down. Ren had said he'd come for me, and I had to trust that he would. Until then, I would do what I'd been taught. What I'd always done.

I would fight.

I would survive.

The darkness came first. It was nothing more than the sensation of clouds moving in front of the sun, and I didn't notice it immediately. But then I started feeling more and more fear. The darkness and the fear went hand in hand.

Conjurite magic. I had to be more vigilant. I had to notice it sooner.

A lock turned in the door, and the large metal door swung open.

Zander stood in front of me.

I gasped when I saw him, my guard against the fear threatening to falter, but I stood, and I forced myself to be strong.

He smirked at me. "Hello, *human.*"

I didn't respond to that. He was trying to use it as an insult.

"Rather human than what you are," I said.

Zander looked surprised. "Cheeky. I don't know if it will save you or get you killed."

"I'm still here, aren't I?"

He chuckled. "Sure. For now."

Dread filled me with those words, but I didn't let it show. Under no circumstances would I let Zander know that I was terrified. I wouldn't let him know I felt anything other than sheer boredom.

I leaned against the wall, forcing myself to look casual so that he didn't know how on edge I was, how close I was to coming undone.

"Where am I?" I asked.

He didn't answer me.

"What do you want with me?"

He sighed. "You ask a lot of questions."

"That happens when I'm left in the dark on a cold cell floor."

Zander chuckled and shook his head. "Your fire is inspiring, little one. It's a pity your light needs to be snuffed out."

29

He was bluffing. I was sure of it. I tried to fight the fear that came with his words and twisted in my gut until I felt sick in my stomach.

But Zander was saying things to work me up, to make my fear worse. It was the game he played. His entire existence was rooted in fear and darkness, and he thrived on it.

He ran his hands through his white-blond hair, and I watched his movement. Before, I had had little of a chance to study him. It was hard to see what someone was capable of when he was attacking me. But the way Zander carried himself, the way he moved, was like that of a warrior.

He knew what he was doing. He knew what he was capable of.

And he would do what was needed, no matter what it took. Loyalty, that was what he'd said to me. I wouldn't underestimate him.

My eyes flitted to the door. It was still open, and not very far from where I stood. Zander was between us, but...

"You won't make it past me," he said, knowing what I was thinking. "But kudos for considering it. It takes courage to want to take someone like me on."

"Yeah?" I asked. "It takes stupidity to kidnap someone like *me*."

Zander laughed. He was amused. He took my threats as entertainment, not for what they really were. I was furious that he'd taken me.

Ren was coming for me. Zander was going to be in a hell of a lot of trouble.

I wanted him to know that. But if he did, he would be ready. Better that he was kept in the dark.

Ha. The male of fear and darkness himself.

"So, you're just going to stand here and laugh at me?" I finally asked. "Or are you here for a reason?"

"I came to check on you, but you seem fine."

"A little hungry, but fine otherwise," I said with a shrug.

He laughed again. "I'll have food sent down. We might wait awhile."

"What are we waiting for?" I asked.

"We're waiting for a guest to arrive." Zander glanced toward the window up above. "And then your time will be up."

He turned and closed the door behind him. When the lock clicked in place and his footsteps faded away, I sagged against the wall and let myself sink onto the rags. I let the fear take over for a moment, trying to breathe through it.

I had to stay strong. I had to keep fighting.

And I had to get the hell out of here if I was going to stay alive. I didn't know who they were waiting for, but I couldn't afford to find out. I needed to get myself to a place where I had a bit of leverage, a way to fight back and protect myself.

In this cell, I would be useless against a Conjurite like Zander. And I knew that if it came down to taking my life, Zander wouldn't hesitate to kill me.

He'd killed Ren's father, after all, and who knows who else?

I looked up at the little window. It was far too high to reach, and it had metal bars that I couldn't remove, even if I climbed the smooth stone walls.

My only way out would be through the door.

I walked to it again. I pressed my hands against it and tried to feel for some kind of magic spell that kept it shut. I'd learned out to discern magic while I'd been training with Dex and Nylah, but I couldn't feel anything.

It was just a heavy metal door with a lock.

I tried throwing myself against it again, but that wouldn't work. It would drain me and hurt me, and that wouldn't do.

I flattened my hands against it and leaned my forehead against the cold metal. Was this all for nothing? Was this where I would end up dying?

It seemed wrong for it all to end when my life had only just started.

My hands started humming, and I frowned. I focused on the strange sensation, and the more I did, the stronger it became. *Magic.*

I thought back to what had happened when I'd been with Nylah. Since then, I hadn't had proof of my magic again. It had shown itself for a moment, only to go away as if it had never been. Nylah had said she sensed Fae magic, but a part of me had refused to believe it.

It seemed so surreal.

There was no denying what I felt now, though. I knew what magic felt like, and this was it.

I wasn't sure what was happening, but I kept my focus on the humming and buzzing in my hands. A moment later, the lock mechanism in the door clicked.

I gasped and stared at the door. I pushed against it, but it wouldn't budge. When I curled my fingers through the slot and pulled, the door groaned and swung open. I stared at the opening, at my freedom, unable to believe what had just happened.

The door was open. And I'd done it.

With magic.

I jerked into motion. I had to get out of here as soon as I could. I could wonder and marvel at what had happened later, when I was safe. Right now, I needed to get away before this Fae that Zander was waiting for arrived and they came back down to find me. If they caught me, it would all be for nothing.

The hallway was long and narrow, made of the same smooth stone as my cell. I passed other cell doors at intervals as I crept quietly along. I was too hurried to peek through the slots and see if other prisoners filled the cells, or to even consider letting them loose.

Right now, I had to save myself, and that was all that mattered.

I was in a dungeon. I'd figured that out when I'd seen the window so high up. When I found a stone staircase winding its way upward, I stepped up. Before I moved on, I stopped and strained my ears for any sound.

No guards stood at their posts, which was strange. Nobody was around. I had to use that to my advantage, but the silence was worrying.

Everything felt wrong. That Conjurite magic was still thick in the air, although Zander wasn't close by. That much, I knew. But I still had to fight the darkness that swirled inside of me as if I had ingested it. Zander must have used it to paralyze me when he'd taken me. But that hadn't been my first encounter with the dark magic, had it? Someone had cast a shape-shifting spell on me. That had to have been Conjurite magic. And Lucia had tried to kill me. Twice. I didn't doubt that she stood with her feet firmly planted in darkness.

The Conjurite magic clung to me, a parasite in my body.

It brought fear with it, but I wouldn't let it consume me. I was *in* darkness. I wasn't *darkness*.

You're stronger than that, I told myself.

I'd been scared in my life many times. I'd been in danger a lot. I knew what it was like to think I was going to die and narrowly escape. This wasn't my first rodeo.

Before I reached the top of the stairs, I heard the clanging of metal armor as someone walked toward me. I panicked and hurried back down the stairs again. At the bottom, there wasn't anywhere to go but the cell I'd escaped from, and I wasn't going back there. I found a dark corner and pressed myself against the wall, trying to become one with the shadows.

A guard came past me, looked up and down the hallway with the doors, and he jingled his keys as if it was a habit to fidget. His eyes flitted over me, but he didn't see me. I held my breath, my heart hammering against my ribs.

He grunted, sat down on a chair, and leaned his head back. The wooden chair groaned under his weight.

When the guard closed his eyes, I made a run for it. I hurried silently and hoped he wouldn't open his eyes before I reached the stairs.

Somehow, I got there without trouble and ran up the stairs. If another guard came down now, I would be screwed.

But there wasn't anyone else. I reached the top of the stairs and looked this way and that. I was in a fortress of sorts, everything built with the same stone than in the dungeon, and it was ugly. The rooms and hallways bore no elegant decorations, no homey touches, nothing that suggested this place was anything other than a prison.

I didn't know which way to go. I didn't know how to get out of here. Staying in one place was going to get me killed or recaptured, so I could figure it out as long as I kept moving.

I chose a direction and moved swiftly, keeping close to the wall. The stone was cold, and I tiptoed to keep my footsteps from echoing on the bare stone floors. The wind howled outside, creating an eerie soundtrack to my escape. Everything around me was monochrome, and the lack of color was unsettling. I kept looking for a dark corner I could hide in if anyone came, but there wasn't anyone in my way.

When I turned the corner again, I felt the darkness too late. I ran right into Zander's muscular chest. I yelped, and he grabbed me by the arms, looking down at me with eyes filled with darkness and rage.

"Well, this is an unexpected twist," a sharp voice said next to me. It scraped along my skin, high pitched and annoying, and it was too familiar.

When I looked at the female, dressed in a beautiful silk gown with hair flowing over her shoulders like a waterfall, it all came together.

"Lucia," I said calmly.

30

Lucia laughed. The sound was as horrible as always, like sandpaper on my skin. This time, I didn't fight the urge to rub my arms and wince.

Her smile faded, draining from her eyes, and she was like a predator. Beautiful, but deadly.

"You're not surprised to see me."

I shook my head.

"What gave me away?"

"The taste of your magic."

She frowned. "In there," she said, tapping Zander's arm and pointing to a door I hadn't noticed.

Zander shoved me toward the door. He dragged me into what looked like a formal sitting room, with hard wooden furniture and uncomfortable looking cushions. The furnishing was in stark contrast to the harsh gray architecture, and it did nothing to make the room cozy.

Zander pushed me onto one seat and stepped away, taking a position a short step away with his arms crossed over his chest like a bodyguard. Lucia sat down in a seat that looked far more comfortable than mine and looked down her nose at me the way she always had.

"I thought you went back to your parents after you left," I said. "I thought..."

I suddenly wasn't sure where I was. Maybe I was in the fortress where she'd grown up. If this place was the life Lucia was used to, being at the palace with Ren must have been like a hotel.

Lucia laughed again.

"You're a fool if you think I'm going to settle for nothing. Far be it from me to let this slide."

I glanced at Zander, who stared at me with his jaw clenched and eyes serious. He was watching me like a hawk, and he was close enough to the door that he would stop me if I tried to make a run for it.

It was exactly what I'd wanted to do, but I pushed the thought out of my mind. I was going to have to escape some other way if I wanted to get away from the two of them.

"So, a Conjurite, huh?"

Lucia rolled her eyes. "Everyone acts like it's such a bad thing." She looked at Zander and smiled before looking at me again.

"It *is* a bad thing," I said. "What good came of it?"

She shook her head. "It takes time to put things in place. Jasfin wasn't built in a day."

"No...but it can be destroyed in one."

Lucia glared at me. "That's not what this is. I don't want to destroy the kingdom. I want to rule it."

"With Zander?" It had been the plan all along. "Did you ever feel anything for Ren?"

She sighed. "You humans and your fantasies. It was a marriage of convenience. Well, it would have been if *you* hadn't ruined the whole thing." Bitterness twisted her face into a scowl. "But no matter, we'll make it work." She held out her hand to Zander, who took it and squeezed briefly.

The contact between them pulsed darkness into the room before it faded again. When they drew apart, I made a mental note; those two together were trouble.

I had to figure out how I was going to get out of here. And for that, I needed her to keep talking. I needed time.

Zander hadn't been willing to monologue his evil plans when he'd attacked me, but Lucia liked it when she looked cunning. She loved herself.

"So, how do you know each other? Did you meet at a Conjurite convention?"

Zander clenched his jaw. Lucia smiled, but it didn't reach her eyes. Under her cute mask, a predator lay in wait to strike.

"Your tongue might get you killed one day."

"And here I thought you would have Zander do it."

She laughed. I *hated* it when she laughed. *Make it stop.* She was a maniac; she needed serious help.

"Zander and I grew up together," she said when her laughter faded.

"So, bonded from the start," I said. "And then you chose the darkness together, too."

"It's beautiful, isn't it?" she asked.

"Romantic."

"When you know someone that well..." She glanced lovingly at Zander. "We've loved each other since we were kids."

"But you were engaged to Ren," I said.

"Yes, yes. That was all part of the plan. To kill King Arnott—which Zander managed incredibly well." She held out her hand to him again, and Zander came closer. She took his hand and pressed it to her lips. He looked proud to be at her side, but she was in control. Did he know he was a puppet? Did he prefer it that way?

"After Ren and I got married, the idea was for Zander to kill him, too. That would put me on the throne, the sad little widow that inherited a kingdom. Zander would join me, then."

I shook my head. How could someone who'd pretended to love Ren do that to him? I remembered all the times she'd called him 'my love.'

"Zander is a Conjurite," I said. "How were you planning to keep him on the throne?"

"I am a master of disguise," Lucia said. "My magic can make anyone take on any form. I hid him all these years, and I can do it again."

I gasped. I'd been turned into Zander and accused of murdering King Arnott. And an assassin had been made to look like Bessie, to kill me.

"It was you?" I asked. "You changed me to look like him? And you... you tried to kill me."

Lucia laughed with glee. "Yes! You figured it out. Oh, it was so hard not to have anyone understand how perfect my plan was, and how well it was working. That was...until you came along."

She glared at me.

"You're the one that put me there," I pointed out. "Why me?"

"It was supposed to be simple. You're the one born with the light." My ears rang when she said those words—the same words Nylah had spoken before Zander had taken me. The start of the prophecy. "Turning you into Zander would have hidden him and taken care of you. But then you slayed the beast, and then Ren took *pity* on you. Poor. Little. Human." She spat the last words like they were poison.

"Something still doesn't add up," I said.

"What?" She looked irritated.

"Why not disguise Zander before he killed King Arnott?"

Lucia's irritation only increased when she glared at Zander. He offered her a stony expression.

"If *someone* wasn't overeager, I might have had a chance."

"It was in the moment," Zander grumbled.

"If you had waited for me..." She took a deep breath and exhaled slowly. "It's fine. It's done."

I shook my head. "You wanted to kill Ren to take the throne, but wouldn't someone from his bloodline inherit the kingdom?"

"You've been doing your reading," Lucia said. "But you forget he has no children. Ren is the last in his line. My family is the next most powerful family in Jasfin. If he died, my family would naturally be next in line to the throne. And, if I were already the widow of the King... nobody would stop me."

Her plan was diabolical. I had to give her that. And to think that she'd been the one to disguise me, to make me look like Zander...

It was hard to wrap my mind around.

"It took a lot of planning, a lot of time putting it all in place. But then you came along and ruined it all. Your bond with Ren is unnatural, Ellie."

"How do you know about that?" I hadn't even known about a bond with him until we'd slept together, and that had been long after Lucia had left.

"Do you think I'm a fool?" she asked bitterly. "I saw it that first day he came to train you. I *felt* it. It was stronger than anything should be between Fae and a human."

I thought back to that first day, when Ren had almost kissed me. We'd connected then, too. But I'd thought it was just me. I'd felt a lot of emotion from him, a connection that had been so much more than anything I'd experienced before. But I hadn't thought too much about it until it had become permanent.

"You tried to kill me after that," I said.

"Can you blame me? They say a jealous female is a terrible thing."

"Jealous?" I asked. "You didn't even love him."

"Does that matter?" Lucia asked.

Zander shifted uncomfortably next to her.

Lucia and Zander were together. I tried to use that.

"It's a crazy story," I said. "Very well-thought out, too."

Lucia looked pleased with herself.

"I can't imagine how you managed it, being away from each other for so long, pretending to love someone else."

"It was a part of the plan," she said with a shrug.

"Sure, I get that. Ren had the enemy right next to him all this time. And you were soaking up all the love and attention he offered. You played the part so well, it was almost as if you felt something for him, too. You had me fooled. Did you sleep with Ren, too?" That last part left a sour taste in my mouth.

Zander was getting angry. It danced in the air like a hot breath. He clenched his jaw, and those dark eyes reflected fiery depths. That was what I wanted. His jealousy fueled his power. I sensed it. His magic was out of control. It wasn't as precise as it had been before.

And fear came along with it. It trembled on my skin, shuddered down my spine.

I swallowed it down. "It takes a lot of love and trust to be together after you've belonged to another male for so long," I said.

Lucia narrowed her eyes. "What are you suggesting?"

"I'm just saying I know how easy it is to fall for Ren. He's the male you can't help but love. And you've been so closely involved with him. I'm surprised it didn't hurt you to walk away."

"Did it?" Zander asked, turning to Lucia.

"What are you talking about?" she replied. "Did what?"

"Did it hurt to walk away from him?" he elaborated. "Did you love him?"

"Of course not," she scoffed. "You know what I was there for."

"But you still got what you wanted while you were there. Win-win, right?"

Lucia stood, furious now, too. "What are you suggesting? That I'm not loyal to you? That I wasn't faithful? We both knew what it would mean. We both understood the sacrifices we had to make to get what we wanted."

Zander shook his head. This was turning into a full-on lover's quarrel.

It was exactly what I wanted.

They continued to fight, magic rising, filling up the room, I shifted closer to the door. If they could keep going for a little longer, I could make a break for it. It would be even better if they didn't notice I was gone for a while.

I almost reached the door when powerful hands grabbed my shoulders and yanked me back.

"Oh, no, you don't," Zander sneered.

I turned around and shoved my palm upward into his nose. He staggered back, caught by surprise. Blood poured out of his nose, and he cursed a string of colorful words. His shock didn't last. His training kicked in, too, and he blocked the next blow and countered it, paired with a wash of magic powerful enough to throw me to the floor.

I cried out, and Zander was on top of me. His hands wrapped around my throat, and this time, it wasn't just magic that strangled me. He snarled at me, his bloodied face horrific, teeth bared, and those fiery eyes promising hell unleashed.

It was real, his skin against mine, his fingers strong.

I made gurgling sounds and clawed at his hands. I tried to kick him. I tried to find whatever magic I had in me, but I was in distress.

My body was freaking out. My vision blurred, and I couldn't think straight with the lack of oxygen anymore.

This was it. It was really over.

I could only cheat death so many times before it caught up with me.

31

The world around me went black, and I let go. I couldn't fight back, and I was tired. Maybe this was it, this was how far I got. I'd been through hell and back, and I'd made it, but what had it all been for?

Only the last couple of months had been worth more than just getting by. And even then, I was just a human in a world where I didn't belong.

Ren was safe. I had exposed Lucia for what she was, and he wouldn't marry her. He might still be in danger, Zander might try to kill him, but at least he knew now who the enemy was. I wished I could have had more time with Ren, but we were never meant to be together. We were too different, and what could I offer as the mate of the all-powerful Fae king?

Not much.

Not much at all.

He would find himself a queen, someone just, true, and kind like he was, someone who could rule with him.

And Nylah...

My heart ached when I thought about the High Priestess. Fierce and powerful and ready to take on the world for her king. And she'd been just as warm and sweet as she'd been strong. She'd become a friend when I hadn't thought I could ever get that close to anyone.

She'd shown me that there were those who cared about each other, just because of who they were, and for no other reason. She'd wanted nothing from me. She'd liked me for who I was.

My mind flashed on the rest of the warriors. Dex, who had trained me to become better and stronger, pushing me past what I'd thought was my own limit. Not being attacked, not being shunned, not being treated as an outcast had been a new sensation. And it had allowed me to believe that I had worth.

They'd all allowed me to believe that.

I filled with warmth when I thought about the Fae I'd come to care for—the Fae I loved.

My mind flashed to Ren once more, and my heart constricted as everything in me went numb.

My fight was over. I was ready to go. I'd finally learned what it was like to love and to be loved in return.

A powerful surge of magic blasted into the room, throwing the door open with a crash. The windowpanes burst into shards that flew outward, and wind whipped through the room.

Before I knew what was happening, a figure shot past me and attacked Zander. Black hair, icy eyes, and a power that was unparalleled rose around me like a giant wave, and through the bond that had solidified between us, I felt Ren's rage.

He'd come for me. He was here.

I pushed up, coughing. I clutched my hand to my throat and tried to relearn how to breathe. My body was on fire as the cells had the oxygen they needed to keep me alive, and I lay limp on the floor, unable to help.

But Ren didn't need my help.

The attack on Zander was ferocious. Ren's lips were curled back in an animalistic snarl. He moved with a motion that seemed almost liquid, every movement precise and deadly. There was no doubt what he was after and what the outcome of the fight would be if Ren succeeded. Zander met the attack with the same fury, and his magic rose to meet Ren's. The clash was like a storm, the dark rumble of

Conjurite magic deafening and the slashes of Ren's magic like light-ning, zapping Zander whenever he tried to make a move. Zander blocked the blows as best he could, but with every blow from Ren, Zander took damage and struggled to counter with the same force.

Lucia screamed, trying to get involved, but Ren's power pushed her against the wall. It held her there, pinned, and she wailed and squealed, fighting her power-fueled bonds. She sounded unhinged, wailing and screeching like a witch about to be burned at the stake.

Ren was far more powerful than Zander, his magic fueled by his anger. Zander's movements were jerky, unrefined compared to Ren's, like a student against a master.

Whatever had happened in the forest when Zander had nearly killed Ren, that wasn't about to happen again. Ren's power was spec-tacular, and Zander didn't stand a chance.

He was going to try, though. He wouldn't give up. Zander was a warrior at heart, and I didn't get the idea that 'surrender' was a word he understood.

"I've had enough of you trying to kill her!" Ren shouted, and his voice boomed in the room. "She's *mine!*"

I shivered. *Mine.*

He slashed at Zander with his bare hand, and a large cut opened across Zander's chest, as if Ren had used a long blade. It was his magic, doing the job better than a sharpened weapon could.

"That's for my father, you lowlife piece of shit!" he yelled.

He sliced him again.

"That's for infiltrating my property and trying to take me out, you treacherous bastard!"

Zander tried to fight back, but Ren's magic overpowered him, and he fell to the floor. There was fear in his eyes when he looked up at Ren. He was finally getting a taste of the fear he'd caused so many to feel during his reign of terror.

"This is for laying a single finger on *my* Ellie!" Ren slashed him across the neck.

Zander's eyes widened, and he moved his mouth, but no words escaped from his lips. He lifted his hand to his throat, but his head fell back before he touched the split skin where blood poured out onto the floor.

His eyes rolled up, and his head lolled to the side, facing me.

When I looked into his eyes, they looked back at me with a vacant stare.

It was over.

Ren stood over Zander, breathing hard.

"No!" Lucia shrieked. She stared in shock. Ren's power let her go— I didn't know if he'd done it on purpose or let go because the fight was over without thinking.

She dropped to the floor and scrambled to her feet.

Now that Zander was dead, the shock turned to horror, and her face twisted in a mask of pain and anguish.

"What have you done?" she cried.

Ren looked up, and when he saw her, he frowned, his face twisting in confusion.

"What the fuck are you doing here?" he demanded.

"You monster!" she shouted, and her hands trembled. Her face changed from horrified to furious. "You've ruined every single thing that mattered to me!" she hissed.

Her power built like static electricity. It danced on my skin and caused the hair in my neck to stand on end and try to march down my spine. The shards of glass on the floor trembled, defied gravity, and floated in the air, held up by her magic. Her hair flew around her head.

She looked like a creature out of this world. Her skin was so tight around her skull, she looked like a living skeleton, and all I could think was that she was the bearer of death.

And she was going to take Ren out.

Her fury was enough to do what needed to be done. For a moment, I wondered if she'd been there, too, if she'd hurt Ren as badly as he'd been hurt when they'd found him in the forest.

"No!" I screamed. I wouldn't allow her to hurt Ren. Not after everything he'd done for me. Not after what I felt for him.

I jumped up and dove in front of Ren.

Lucia was like a ball of energy, building and building, and she spontaneously combusted. I was in front of Ren when the power came at us. There was no time to think, no time to wonder what I was and what I could do. All I knew was that I had to protect him.

My power was at the surface. I could feel it humming and buzzing. I grabbed it and yanked it out, and suddenly, the room was filled with light. I was at the center, magic pouring out of me. I created a shield before me, a net that caught everything Lucia threw at me. It caught the power and held fast. The humming and buzzing increased. Every nerve ending was alive, and the power was so strong I felt like it might pull me apart. I absorbed everything she had, catching it at first, and when she stopped throwing it at me, I started taking it from her.

She screamed, her voice becoming higher and higher, the pitch like a shattering whine that sliced through everything.

The furniture in the room trembled, danced in place, fell over. It moved around the room, as if an earthquake rattled the very foundations of the fort we were in.

When I couldn't take any more of it, when the power was so much, I felt like I would burn out or explode—a supernova—the magic cracked and shattered.

Lucia screamed as waves of hot magic washed over her, tearing at her hair, her clothes, her skin.

An explosion blasted everything away from us. The wooden furniture crashed and splintered against the walls. The walls cracked. The floor split open, shifting, shaking until a crevice gaped across the floor. Then, it stopped.

I sank to my knees, all the energy gone out of me. A fine dust covered everything, and from the gaping cracks, a cold wind forced its way in.

"Ellie!" Ren cried out and caught me as I sagged to the floor.

I didn't know how long I'd been out for. When I opened my eyes, Ren sat on the floor, cradling me against his chest. He stroked my hair, rocking back and forth.

"Ellie!" he gasped when I looked up at him. "What the hell were you thinking?"

"That I would not let you die."

He shook his head. "You nearly got yourself killed. What would I do then? What—"

I stared up at this male who was about to lose it over nearly losing *me*.

"I'm still here," I said. "It's not so easy to get rid of me."

A laugh bubbled up in his throat, and his relief washed over me.

"No, I see that. You're impossible to kill."

He smiled at me, and I could have sworn I saw a shimmer of tears in his eyes. But he blinked it away.

"When you disappeared, I thought it was over. I thought I'd lost you. And my world ended, Ellie. Everything I've fought for, everything I've worked for... None of it matters if you're not with me."

"You've lived for centuries without me."

He ran his fingers down my cheek. "Only because I didn't know you. Now that I've tasted life with you, I can't go back to how it was. The thought of losing you..." He shuddered at the horror he'd experienced, and waves of that horror flowed over me. I could sense his distress, how terrified he'd been of losing me.

I lifted my hand and touched his cheek.

"I'm empty without you," he said. "Ellie, you're everything."

"I'm not going anywhere," I told him. Ren and I belonged together. We were from different walks of life. He was Fae, and I was human. We had more obstacles than anyone to overcome to be together. But if it was what we both wanted, then I would fight every day to be at his side.

"You faced the monster," Ren said.

"I would fight a thousand Lucias for you," I answered.

He lowered his head and kissed me.

Dex ran into the room, a slew of warriors following him. They were bloodied and looked like they'd fought an entire war just to get into the fortress. Zita was among them, her face dirty, and blood was caked in her short blonde hair. She grinned at me when she saw me in the King's arms.

"Looks like you guys have it under control in here."

Nylah followed right behind them, and her eyes widened when she saw the surrounding carnage.

She trod carefully into the room, looking at everything as if studying a crime scene.

"There was a lot of magic here," she said.

Ren nodded. "Yes. A lot of magic." He didn't take his eyes away from me. "Who knew you had it in you?"

"I don't know what it was," I said, my voice trembling.

"It's who you are," Nylah said. "You just needed a reason to unleash your power within."

A reason. I'd had a hell of a reason to find what I was capable of. If I'd lost Ren, if he died, even if it was for me, I would never have been able to recover from that. I loved him.

I wouldn't let him die.

Ren stood and walked to Zander's body.

"Is that really him?" Dex asked.

Ren knelt next to Zander, and I felt, rather than saw, how he searched the male with his magic. Finally, he nodded.

"It's him. Zander is truly dead. My father's death has been avenged."

His sorrow became my own. He could finally find his peace now and deal with his father's death, knowing that justice had been brought to the killer.

His father was still gone, and Ren still had a long road of grieving ahead, but he could at last let his father rest in peace.

Ren stood and came to me. His face was filled with compassion that washed the sorrow on his features away. He held out his hand, and it was more than just a hand to help me up. When I touched him, here in the middle of the carnage, with the broken glass and blood on the floor and Lucia's ashes blowing around, touching Ren was like coming home.

"Come," Ren said, helping me up. "Let's get you out of here." He looked at Nylah for the first time. "Will you take care of the rest?"

"I will," she said. "Dex and I have this covered."

Dex grunted something I couldn't understand, and Ren stood, lifting me in his arms. He turned, and the guards stepped aside, making a way for him to carry me out of the room. I didn't remember making our way out of the fortress or how we went back to the palace. I couldn't remember how I'd ended up in Ren's bedroom. All I knew was that it was over. The threat was gone.

And we all lived.

🦋 33 🦋

I slept. I didn't know how long, but I was buried in Ren's bed for what felt like days. Sometimes, when I woke to go to the bathroom, he was right here with me. And sometimes, he was somewhere else, running the kingdom. But he was always just a thought away, and when I needed him, he appeared as if I'd summoned him without knowing it.

After sleeping like the dead, I felt better for the first time since everything had happened.

Ren sat on the edge of the bed, smiling at me when I blinked my eyes open.

"I think I slept for years," I said, covering my face. I was pretty sure I looked like crap, too. Sleeping Beauty had been beautiful after sleeping for a century, but my hair was a tangled mess.

"You needed it," Ren said with a chuckle. "Don't cover your face. You're beautiful."

I warmed at his words.

"I like you in my bed," he growled.

I giggled and pushed up so that I sat.

"How long did I sleep for?" I asked.

"Two days," Ren said.

I gasped. "I missed training."

He laughed. "I'll write you a note to excuse you from class." He winked at me. "Dex will be fine with it."

I laughed, too, shaking my head. "I don't know why I was so tired."

"You used a lot of magic, Ellie," Ren said. "That's bound to wear anyone out, especially if you're not used to it."

"It was a lot," I said, nodding slowly. "I didn't know... How do I have so much magic?"

"I don't know," Ren confessed. "I won't pretend that I have any idea what's happening, but we'll find out. Nylah is on it, and it doesn't matter how long it takes, we're going to figure it out. I can't tell you how relieved I am that you have it, though."

I looked at my hands and nodded. "Makes me a better warrior, right?"

Ren put his hand on mine. "It means you're still alive...and so am I."

His eyes were serious when he looked at me. He'd been terrified of losing me.

"When I saw Zander's hands wrapped around your throat, I lost it," Ren admitted. "I thought you were already gone, and I can't explain to you how that broke me." As he talked, the pain that it had brought him to think that he'd lost me was like heartburn in my chest.

"I'm here," I said, squeezing his hand. "I'm safe."

Ren nodded. "Yeah. We'll find out what's going on, and we'll teach you how to use your magic." He leaned his forehead against mine. I closed my eyes, and I felt our connection, stronger than ever. "Something like this will never happen again. I won't let it."

"How did you know where to find me?" I asked. "And how did you know I was calling out for you?"

"It's our bond," he said, cupping my cheek and looking into my eyes. "It helped us communicate over the distance. Ever since we slept together, I've been able to sense your feelings, and when you called out to me, I knew where you were. All I had to do was follow it until I found you."

"Thank you," I said. "For coming for me."

"Not coming for you would have been like letting a part of myself die, Ellie."

I shivered at the words, and the warmth of his love washed over me.

"I think I need to have a shower," I said. "And something to eat."

"I'll call for food. Shower, and come back to me."

I nodded, climbed out of bed, and headed to the shower. When I emerged from the bathroom, drying off with a towel, Ren came to me and kissed me.

"Whatever this is, we'll work through it together," he said. "I don't know what it all means, but I know I never want to be apart from you again. What I feel for you..." He struggled to find the words, but I *felt* it through the bond. "That is, if you will have me. I've been such an idiot about this bond and not seeing it for what it was. I should have known better." He bit the inside of his cheek, and a strand of his black hair fell over his brow. "Will you stay? Not as a warrior, but with me? I need you more than I have ever needed anything."

I shook my head. "I want both. I want to be with you, Ren. I'm in love with you. But I don't want to give up fighting. I want to fight by your side, so we can take on whatever comes our way as a team."

Ren nodded. "I didn't think you could take care of yourself before. I was very wrong. You've proven, yet again, that the strength you possess knows no bounds."

He leaned in and kissed me again, his hand cupping my cheek. His body was so close, heat radiated from him, threatening to consume me. His need echoed my own, heat rising inside me to match his.

I lost myself in the kiss and dropped the towel to the floor. Ren's tongue slipped into my mouth, and he guided me back to the bed. I sighed when he rolled against me, his body half-pinning me to the mattress.

His hands roamed my body, and I let my hands run down his back, too. His muscular body was enormous, and I could barely reach around him. I held onto his broad shoulders. The muscles in his back moved under my fingers as he did, and I shivered when he ground his hips against me. He was rock hard and eager, and I was as ready for him as he was for me.

My nipples were erect with lust, and when he tweaked them and kneaded and massaged my breasts, I cried out in pleasure.

I reached into Ren's pants and wrapped my fingers around his shaft. He gasped, and I pumped my hand up and down, my fingers getting slick with the lust oozing out of his tip.

His lips were still locked on mine, but he broke the kiss, and we let go of each other long enough for him to undress. His erection sprung free, and he was *delicious* to look at.

I nudged him onto his back and straddled his legs. When I glanced up at him, his eyes were filled with lust.

I sat on his legs and pumped his cock with my hands a few times before I lowered my head and sucked him into my mouth. While I did, sucking him in as far as he would go, I cupped his balls and gently massaged him. I relished in the moans and groans that came from his lips as he pushed his hands into my hair. He held it in fists and encouraged me to take him deeper, to suck harder, until he shivered and trembled and pushed me away.

"Sorry," he gasped. "I'm going to lose it."

I nodded and crawled over him. I straddled him, and he guided his cock toward my entrance as I lowered my hips. I moaned when he pushed into me, and I sank down with a groan. I gasped as I shifted and adjusted to his size. It felt like he'd grown even larger overnight.

When I was ready, I started moving. I rocked my hips back and forth, sliding him in and out of me.

Ren cupped my breasts, fondling them while I slowly rode him. His eyes were riddled with need, but I was going to tease him.

I moved achingly slow—so slowly it frustrated me, too. But I wanted to draw this out good and long. I wanted to feel every inch of him and savor every second we had together.

"You're driving me crazy," he said, lips parted, breathing hard.

"Yeah?" I asked, lowering myself and kissing him.

He nodded against me. His hands slid down my sides, and he grabbed my hips, rocking me back and forth harder and harder.

I giggled. "That's cheating."

"What you're doing to me is cheating," he grunted.

I bucked my hips harder and faster, the way he was urging me to do. I started riding him, my breasts jiggling, and Ren stared at them now and then before he locked eyes with me, reminding me that this was all about me and our connection, and not just the pleasure.

The bond between us was strong. His need for me, his desperate ache to have all of me, flowed through it. But I felt his affection, the purity of his love for me just as strongly. And I relished in that feeling, knowing that he felt it, too.

My clit rubbed against his pubic bone as I rocked harder and harder, and I was well on the way to my first orgasm. The pleasure started building inside of me, and the combination of the friction against my clit and his thick cock deep inside of me, rubbing up against all the right places, brought me closer and closer to the edge.

When I orgasmed, ecstasy erupted at my core, and I collapsed on his chest, giving myself over to the sexual bliss that crashed down on me like waves on the shore. I cried out and moaned, my fingers digging into Ren's arms where I held on for dear life. If I wasn't tethered to him, I felt like I would break free and float away.

The orgasm was intense, but it was short-lived. When it passed, I breathed hard.

I lifted my head, and Ren brushed my hair out of my face. His eyes filled with affection.

Without warning, he rolled over, holding onto me, and suddenly, I was beneath him. I was still breathing hard, body humming in the aftermath of my orgasm, but Ren pulled back and pushed into me again. He moved slowly at first, knowing that I was sensitive, my body tight after the orgasm. He picked up his pace after a while of making sure I was fine and bucked his hips harder and harder.

I cried out as he pounded into me, and I grabbed onto his muscular shoulders as if I would fall if I let go. I looked into his eyes, and his face was a mask of lust and concentration.

His strokes shortened, and he picked up his pace yet again. He hammered into me, my body rocking on the bed, my naked rubbing against his chest.

A second orgasm grew inside me, building and building until I knew I would fall apart if he kept pushing.

And he did. His hips bucked against mine, and I cried out when his efforts exploded into the second orgasm. It started at my core and washed out to my extremities, and I felt like I was made of light. When I opened my eyes, the room was illuminated by the bright light that bled from my skin.

Ren cried out sharply, thrust deeply into me, and he jerked and pulsed inside of me as he released, filling me up even more.

His eyes were on me, and they glowed with an echo of the light that consumed me.

This didn't happen when I orgasmed alone, but it happened when we orgasmed together. And whatever it was, if it was a product of me and Ren, I was happy with it. We were perfect together, him and I.

We rode out our orgasms together, our bond connecting us as one. When it was finally over, Ren collapsed onto the bed next to me. He pulled me tightly against him.

"I love being this close to you," he said, stroking my skin. The glow was slowly fading as the orgasm did.

"Me too," I said, still gasping and panting.

We lay together in silence for a while, enjoying being so close to each other, not needing any words to explain what we felt. Because we could both feel it. For ourselves, and for each other.

"I wish I knew what it was," I finally said.

I turned to look at Ren.

His eyes were closed, but his fingers stroked my hair, and his brows were knitted together.

"Me too. But we'll find out."

His confidence set me at ease. We had a lot of questions and very few answers. But we were together, and he was serious when he said he wanted to be with me. I wanted it, too. All of it.

Ren was an incredible male. Not only a good king, but a wonderful male. He'd come for me when I'd needed him. He'd been willing to fight for me to the death, and we'd gotten through the worst together. Zander—the male who'd killed Ren's father—was dead. Lucia was gone as well.

There was no danger, now. Everything was going to be okay.

My mind drifted to Ren, and I wondered what our future would hold. I still had a lot of questions, but one thing was for sure.

This was where I belonged.

34

We sat at breakfast with Nylah and Dex a few days later. We'd been spending more time together, the four of us. I felt like I was a part of the family, not only a warrior fighting in the King's name.

For the first time in my life, I had a home.

The plates were empty; the servants had cleared away the leftover food, and we sat in companionable silence after a substantial breakfast.

Shouts were heard from outside the doors, and we all stiffened.

Before any of us could react, the doors to the dining room burst open, and a male and a female marched in with an air of importance. Servants bustled around them.

"His lordship Baut, and his lady Carlin, Your Highness," the servant said and bowed.

I frowned. The servants treated them as if they belonged. Ren didn't look surprised to see them, either. Weariness flowed through our bond, but not surprise.

Magic crackled in the surrounding air.

Baut had dark brown hair, cropped short, and a beard that gave him an intimidating look. The female at his side, Carlin, had lighter hair, blonde with streaks of white. They both had cerulean eyes that were filled with anger. They looked young, but with Fae, you never could tell. They could be thirty or three thousand years old.

"Baut," Ren said. "You came at an inconvenient time. If you had announced your arrival, I would have prepared a meal and set time aside to talk." He sighed and looked at the male, who wore a dashing suit embellished with golden chains and jewels. Clearly, they knew each other well enough that Baut and Carlin had been allowed into the palace as esteemed guests.

"It couldn't wait," Baut said tightly.

Nylah shifted a little closer and leaned in.

"Those are Lucia's parents," she whispered.

My blood ran cold.

"You have some nerve sitting there like the cowardly king that you are, talking to me that way when you're the reason my daughter is dead!"

"Let's talk in my office," Ren said calmly.

"Oh, no, you don't. I want this conversation here and now, where everyone can hear what's being said. Where there are witnesses to this injustice."

His fury crackled around us in the room. There was an undercurrent of magic, but it didn't feel like a threat. I was uncomfortable, shifting in my seat.

I'd killed Lucia. They were mad at Ren, but it was my fault.

"All right, we'll talk here," Ren said. "Where there are witnesses. If you like, I can call for a scribe to take it all down."

Baut spat. "Did you think you were going to get away with this? You might be the King, but murder is murder!"

Ren shook his head. "I did you a favor by letting you know what happened. I didn't have any obligation to do it, but we've been friends for a long time, and you were in good standing with my father. Don't expect me to extend any more liberties. Lucia's actions brought her fate upon herself."

"Lies!" Baut shouted. His anger was getting the better of him. Ren was calm. "I reject your excuses. Lucia was your fiancée! Do you think it's any less treacherous to turn on her in her death?"

I wanted to cry out that she'd turned on Ren. That she'd never been on his side. But Nylah, sensing my frustration, put her hand on my arm to keep me quiet. I bit my tongue and watched Ren handle it all with grace. He didn't throw them out, as was his right, and he didn't lose his temper with the male shouting at him like that, either.

"Lucia sealed her own fate when she became a Conjurite," Ren said. "She planned to kill me, as she and Zander had killed my father. Even without what happened, that is a crime punishable by death. There isn't much more I can do about that. She would have died either way."

Baut looked like he was going to explode. His anger was so thick in the air, I could almost choke on it.

"I won't have your excuses, *boy*!" he yelled.

"Do I need to remind you that I'm your king?" Ren asked. "I may have extended you special privileges with how you address me in private, but I'm your ruler, and I will be given the respect that comes with it."

"Respect? Ha! What a joke! You don't deserve respect. Not when you chose *her* over my Lucia and concocted this lie about Lucia siding with a Conjurite to get rid of her!" He pointed a finger at me.

My jaw dropped.

"How could you?" Carlin asked, talking for the first time. Her words trembled like she wanted to cry, and my heart went out to her. No matter how evil Lucia had been, Carlin had lost a daughter. "If you'd just kept her in your life... Instead, you chose a *human* over her."

She glared at me, spitting the word as if it was a curse word. Baut scowled at me.

They hated me. That much was clear. Not because of Lucia's death, which I was to blame for, but because of who I was.

"You have no say over my choices," Ren said. He wasn't getting angry with them; he wasn't shouting back at them.

It was impressive. I would have lost my calm a long time ago.

"You can't be with her," Carlin said.

"I can do as I please."

"You're putting everyone in danger," she insisted. "The prophecy is clear."

We all froze and stared at her.

"You know about the prophecy?" I asked in a thin voice.

Ren glanced at me. "Carlin is a priestess. She has access to the Goddess Terra and the prophecies that are foretold."

"Priestess," Nylah said, not without reverence. I wouldn't have talked to her that way after how they'd barged in, but everyone was being painfully polite. "What did you see? Please, share with us, so that we may be enlightened."

"I'm not helping *you*," Carlin said. "You're more powerful than I am. If you don't know..." She shook her head in disgust. "But I will tell you this." She looked at Ren. "If you allow this cretin to rule, it will bring the world as we know it to destruction."

This wasn't the first time I was referred to as a creatin, and I didn't appreciate it.

I wanted to say as much, but Nylah tightened her grip on my arm.

"We have nothing more to say," Ren said. "I am saddened by your loss. I know the pain of losing a loved one." I could see on his face that he really meant it; he was sorry that Lucia's parents had suffered, even if it had been Lucia's fault. "There is nothing more I can do for you. I must ask you to leave."

"This isn't over, Rainier," Baut said. A steely determination replaced his anger. "I won't let this go. You can't take action and expect to leave everyone in your wake to be pleased with what you do. The choices you make as king will create enemies. And you've made an enemy out of me."

"I'm sorry to hear that," Ren said, and again, I knew how honest he was being. "I hoped we could put this nasty business behind us."

After all, Baut and Carlin, as hurt as they were about their daughter, didn't have a foot to stand on. Lucia had betrayed Rainier and planned his death. She would have been executed had she not been killed.

But Ren was a kind Fae, and he wanted to give them pardon. They hadn't played a role in it all.

Baut shook his head. "You'll be sorry when I wage war against you."

"Careful, Baut. You're dangerously close to the edge."

"Do I look like I don't know what I'm saying? Half the kingdom is on my side. Do you think they'll trust you, now that you chose a human to rule by your side?"

"A human who will bring certain destruction to the Fae lands," Carlin added.

Ren shook his head, and his anger flared up inside him. "I am still king. If you wage war against me, it's treason, and I will have to treat you and anyone that follows you as hostile."

"Treat me however you like. Nothing can be worse than ripping our daughter away from us. This is war, Ren. It's not over."

"How dare you threaten me?" Ren hissed. His voice was bitter, his eyes so light they were almost white. "Guards!"

Guards burst into the room, ready to obey the King's orders.

"You are under arrest for treason."

Baut turned around, his magic at his fingertips, and the atmosphere became so loaded with power I couldn't breathe. He pulled his lips back into a snarl and glared at the guards, willing them to come for him. He was ready to fight—he was enraged and hungry for blood.

Guards charged him, but Baut threw power at them. The warriors were prepared, though—they'd trained with Dex, after all.

They countered, and in almost no time, they were on Baut.

"Baut!" Carlin cried out, jumping to his side. A new power rose—it was like Nylah's power, but something about it reminded me of Lucia.

Carlin grabbed her husband, yanking him toward the window. Magic rose and burst out from her in the blink of an eye. Next to me, Nylah's power rose to counter it, but the windows shattered, and Carlin and Baut stepped toward them...and disappeared.

The guards breathed hard, looking around the room.

"They're gone," Dex said.

"Damn priestess magic," Ren grumbled.

Nylah shook her head. "I didn't expect that. I should have known they would do something."

I stared at the spot where they'd vanished, stunned.

"Oh, Goddess," Nylah whispered under her breath and dropped her head into her hand.

Dex's face was grim, his lip pursed into a thin line.

The guards left with the threat gone, and we were left in the after-math. I reeled with what I'd just seen, with what had just been said.

Ren sat down with a sigh. "That was unnecessary." He rubbed his forehead with his fingertips.

"Will they really wage war?" I asked, lowering myself into my seat again.

He nodded. "They're furious about Lucia's death. I tried to reason with them after we got back, but there's nothing as dangerous as a male who is convinced beyond all reason that he's right."

"But...what does it mean? The prophecy she talked about? Destruction..."

My heart sank, and I filled with dread. It had been a lot to swallow, finding out that I wasn't fully human. But to think that I was bad, that my existence would bring destruction? I scrubbed my face with my hands, trying to figure it out.

"She didn't say what the prophecy was. There would be only two reasons to hide it," Nylah said. She tried to sound reassuring, but I could tell she was as rattled as I was. "Either she won't tell us every-thing because it's not true, or she doesn't know."

"Whichever it is," Ren said, "we'll find out."

"We will," Nylah assured. "You shouldn't worry about it. We'll do it together."

It was easy to tell me not to worry. It was easy to say everything was going to be fine. But what if it wasn't? What if I really was a prob-lem? The last thing I wanted was to hurt anyone, to do what Lucia had done.

Even if it was unintentional.

"Don't," Ren said, knowing my thoughts. "You're not like her. And I don't believe it. Not for a second."

I swallowed and nodded. "Okay."

"We're taking this one step at a time," Nylah said.

"That's right," Ren agreed.

"What's the first step?" I asked.

Ren was grim when he answered.

"We prepare for war."

❦

Continue Reading the Fate of the Fae Series

Book Two: Forbidden Fae
Women like me don't get to live happily ever after.

The Fae King claims me as his own, but a fairytale ending is not in my foreseeable future. Half of the kingdom supports our union. The other half of the kingdom wants to hunt me down.

I keep getting visions, and I must run to escape that possible truth. How am I supposed to convince the kingdom I'm not evil? I can't even convince myself.

My unique power and the prophecy that surrounds it are mysteries nobody understands.

I don't know what darkness resides in me. I don't know how to find the light.

There's only one way to escape this, even though it's the last thing I want to do.

Download on Amazon now!

VERA RIVERS BOOKS

Receive a FREE romance ebook by visiting my website and signing up for my mailing list:

VeraRiversAuthor.com

By signing up for our mailing list, you'll receive a FREE ebook. The newsletter will also provide information on upcoming books and special offers.

OTHER BOOKS YOU'LL LOVE

Midlife Magic and Mates
Magic. Mayhem. Hot alphas that rock their worlds.

Not bad for women in their forties.

Join forces with Molly, Stephanie, Ali, and Missy as they soar into their forties with newfound magic and romance!

Fate of the Fae
In the world of the Fae, it's hard to know who to trust.
Follow the fated romance of Ellie and Rainier as they fight the Conjurites to survive and save their kingdom.

Printed in Great Britain
by Amazon

11433473R10123